HER BULL RIDER'S BABY

GENEVIEVE TURNER

LILIANA MERRILL STARED AT THE plastic stick sitting on her toilet lid, her brain not quite believing what her eyes were telling her.

It wasn't real. She wouldn't let it be real.

Bea would confirm that this was all a terrible dream. Lil wrenched open the bathroom door and called to her cousin in the other room. "What does two stripes mean again?"

Beatriz shuffled to the bathroom door but didn't peep in. "You know exactly what two stripes mean," she called back. "Are you done?"

Liliana didn't let the edge of irritation in Beatriz's voice upset her. It *had* been kind of a dumb question, and Bea had little patience for those. In Lil's defense, finding out she was pregnant was scrambling her thoughts.

Pregnant. Now she got why people said a pause was pregnant—this was some heavy, chest-flattening stuff. She sucked in a breath, looked again at the stick. Still two stripes. *Damn.*

"I'm done." *I'm toast.*

Beatriz propped herself in the doorway, her razored bob

as stick straight as the rest of her and as dark as her stylish clothes.

Liliana waved the stick under her nose. "Can you double-check that there are two lines? Look closely." Maybe she was seeing double? Definitely better to have something wrong with her eyesight than to be pregnant.

"I'm not handling your pee stick." Bea leaned as far away as she could without falling over backward. "And yes, there're two."

Someone other than Liliana would have found her cousin's attitude off-putting. Not platitudes, no assurances that everything would be okay, no nonsense—only simple practicality. Lil actually found it comforting. She needed to cling to Bea's calmness or else she'd freak out.

Bea had seen two lines too. *Okay. Ooookay.*

"Two lines," Lil said weakly, holding tighter to her illusion of being totally cool. *A baby. She was going to have a baby.*

She tossed the stick into the trash. No need for that anymore—those two lines were burned into her retinas. She sank down onto the closed toilet, putting her head in her hands. The denim of her jeans was suddenly unbearably scratchy, her ropers too heavy for her feet. Her coolness was rapidly melting under the realization that it was really real.

A baby. A real live baby.

"Hey, Lil." Bea's tone was gentler but still brisk. "Lots of people have babies. It's not the end of the world."

In other words: *Buck up, little camper.*

Bea was right, but Lil kind of wanted to pretend like the world was ending if only for a few moments. "I can't have a baby. I have a job. A career." She raised her arms to the heavens, toward the uncaring Fates who'd done this to her.

Her cousin rolled her eyes behind the heavy black

frames of her glasses. "Pregnant women work in labs all the time. I saw one yesterday."

"I'm not a scientist. I don't work in a lab." Lil flicked her ponytail over her shoulder—even her hair was annoying her. "I run a stock operation, and I'm trying to breed bucking bulls. How many pregnant women work with over a thousand pounds of testosterone-soaked bull, purposefully trying to piss him off so he'll buck?"

Bea might be the smart one in the family, but suggesting that Lil keep on with the bull program she was setting up wasn't a genius move.

"You won't be pregnant forever. Put the bull-breeding stuff on hold and focus on the stock operations until the baby comes." Bea's tone was smugly self-assured.

What her cousin suggested made perfect sense. Yet... Lil didn't want to heed the advice. The stock operations were an inherited duty, passed down from Merrill to Merrill for over a century, and now it was Lil's turn to run them. She had to keep the operations going in order to hand them off to the next generation.

There was more than enough work in running them to keep anyone busy. But Lil just had to make things harder for herself. So she'd decided to start a bull-breeding operation. Something new, something all hers, not passed down from anyone. It was going to be Liliana's baby.

"We're already building the facility. The lab, the barn, the training pen and chutes—I don't want to let it sit for months. This bull program... It was going to be all mine. I wasn't going to be just another Merrill taking over what her daddy gave her. I'm building something all my own."

When she'd taken over the stock operations of the family ranch, the rodeo world had been grudgingly accepting. The old-timers might have preferred to keep working with her father, but Lil was William Merrill's little girl, and keeping things in the family was always best. Her party-girl reputation didn't help matters, but she was young and she worked hard during the day—she deserved to blow off steam come nightfall. The older crowd might frown about it, but they'd never chided her openly.

That all changed when she announced her intention to start breeding and training bulls—the disapproval had been open and vocal. William Merrill's little girl had no business messing with bucking bulls, and people weren't afraid to tell her that to her face, to tell her no repeatedly.

Being pregnant while messing with bucking bulls? The disapproval would create a cloud of smog bigger than the one covering LA. If she lost all her goodwill in the rodeo community, her bull operation would be sunk.

She tugged on her ponytail. All that money she was spending on this bull-breeding facility, telling her brothers she was so certain the program would start to pay off... She chewed on her lip. If things kept on as they had, she'd have nothing to show for her work except a pile of debt. She had to turn the breeding program around.

"It will still be all your own in a few months." Bea leaned into the bathroom, a frown pinching her brow. "But you could... well, you know."

Lil knew. That possibility sat at the back of her mind. She'd always wanted children someday. Someday—but not today.

She had so many plans for the stock operations, things she wanted accomplished *before* settling down. How many of her dreams would she have to give up for the baby?

She set her hands to her belly. There was another life in there, growing and changing within her. *An entirely new person.*

Her head spun. The baby was within her, yet was already something completely outside her. It almost sounded like a... a miracle.

Lil blinked, took a sharp breath. *This* was the next generation she had to pass the ranch to. This baby inside her—this was a new Merrill. Lil had an almost sacred duty to raise this baby in the ranching lifestyle, to prepare it for when it would take over whatever part of the ranch he or she was called to. That was what the Merrills and Morenos and even the Spencers did.

They ran the Ranch.

Lil shook her head, sat up straighter. "No. I couldn't."

It would be easier to do that, but she couldn't. Lil sighed. She always had to make things harder for herself, didn't she?

Bea raised an eyebrow. "Are you sure? Once you decide, there's no undoing it."

Easy for Bea to say; that wasn't her pee stick in the trash. "You can't even say the word," Lil said. "What makes you think I could do it?"

"Okay, that option's out." Bea crossed her arms. "Congratulations then. You're going to have a baby."

Lil let her head fall forward. There was that weight again, flattening the sense of wonder and miraculousness. *Pregnant.* "Thanks." About as glum and ungracious as a thank-you could get. It might be a miracle, but it sure was an inconvenient one. Of all the times for her to get knocked up...

"The bull-breeding operation isn't going quite as well as I might have made it sound," she admitted to her cousin.

"How is that? Bull meets cow, they fall in love, and make a calf. Simple."

"Not quite." Lil rubbed at her jeans. "I sent the selection

committee videos of two of our best bulls last week. Really, really great bulls. And they said no. Wouldn't even consider them for the junior rodeo circuit." Her voice was flat, but her temper when she'd gotten the refusal had been anything but. She'd ranted and raged because she knew it was just a bullshit excuse to keep those bulls out of the rodeo—a way to get back at her for daring to do what they considered unladylike.

She'd written five scathing e-mails, then deleted them all. Pissing off the committee wasn't going to win this fight. But it had been damn hard to hit that Delete key instead of the Send button.

"Well, I am very sorry," Bea said, although it was clear from her tone she didn't quite know what that meant. "But you can try again, right?"

"Yeah." Lil didn't get into the specifics. It was going to take more than trying again—it was going to take a bull that even they couldn't ignore. She could breed that bull, she just knew it. She'd prove them all wrong in the end. She only had to get to that end.

Bea took a deep breath, as if hesitant, which was weird because her cousin considered herself to always be one hundred percent correct. "Do you know who the father is?"

Lil snapped up off the toilet seat, her boot heels clattering against the floor. "Of course I do."

He has tiger eyes. Eyes that had gleamed with a predator's golden intent...

Bea was not going to be impressed by that.

"You don't have a boyfriend," Bea pointed out. "It's not as if there's a likely suspect."

True. Lil didn't have time to date. Men were for fun, for spending reckless, sweaty nights with. Not for messing about with during the day doing relationship stuff. She had a business to run—she didn't have time for that.

But she hadn't slept with anyone since Vegas. Which was how she knew exactly who the father was.

"So," Bea prompted with mockery shading her tone, "who is it?"

Liliana rubbed her forehead. "We met in Vegas."

"Wait." Bea's mouth fell open. "Is this... *tiger eyes*?"

Heat crawled into Liliana's cheeks. Bea had been talking to their other cousin Penny then.

When she'd called him Tiger Eyes, she'd meant the gemstone because it captured his eyes perfectly—deep brown banded with lush stripes of gold, a color that had taken her breath away.

The nickname had been funny when he'd been an encounter in Vegas, a story to sigh over as she shared beers with Penny.

But now he was the father of her baby.

He'd always been much more than an encounter. He'd consumed her nights and her days during that heady weekend. Which was why she hadn't been interested in anyone else since. Not that she advertised that.

She was fun-loving, wild Liliana. She couldn't be tied down. Getting hung up on a bull rider she'd met at the National Finals Rodeo? Totally not her style.

Now she was pregnant. Talk about getting hung up.

"But wait..." Bea's brow furrowed, and Lil could see her doing the math. "Vegas was three months ago. And you're only now taking the test?"

"Yeah. I didn't miss my period until last week." Lil rubbed her forehead. Of course her body had to be one in a million and have a period while she pregnant. She just had to make things harder for herself.

"Then how do you know Tiger Eyes is the dad?" No censure from Bea, only puzzlement.

"Because I haven't slept with anyone since." He'd kind of ruined men for her after that wild weekend. She gave a soft laugh. And now she was about to ruin all kinds of things for him.

"Ah. Does he have a name, or should I keep calling him Tiger Eyes?"

"His real name is Adriano," Lil confessed.

Bea's brow furrowed. "A bull rider named Adriano?" She clapped a hand over her mouth. "Oh my God. Lil, he's so famous even I've heard of him."

"Yep."

Adriano Silva. Young, Brazilian, and the most famous up-and-coming bull rider in America.

And father to a baby he didn't even know about. How was he going to feel about that?

"He was in *Style Magazine*." Bea actually flapped her hands she was so excited.

Liliana clamped hers together because she was most definitely not excited. "*Style?* That doesn't really seem like his style." She winced at the unintentional joke.

Adriano had seemed completely focused on bull riding and none of the other trappings that came with it. No interviews, no excessive rumors of him with buckle bunnies, no late-night carousing.

But when their eyes had locked across the arena, he'd been completely focused on *her*. And she on him.

But Vegas was Vegas, and real life was real life. When those days of crazy hot sex had been over, she hadn't tried to call him. There'd been no call from him. They'd both gone back to reality.

Bea grabbed her hand, pulled her out of the bathroom.

"Come on. We can't keep discussing this while you're less than a foot from the toilet."

Because being ten feet away from it would somehow make all this better? But she followed Bea into the living room and let her cousin settle her onto the couch.

Lil stared at the coffee table. She still had to tell her family.

Oh God. She rubbed at her suddenly sour belly. Her parents would likely be happy—ever since they'd retired, they'd been subtly hinting that their children needed to settle down and make some grandbabies. But they hadn't meant for Lil do it like this.

And her brothers... Luke would come around. Probably. She was pretty good at convincing him about stuff.

Benedict—Benedict wasn't so easily swayed. Being the eldest, he took his role as leader of the family seriously. As seriously as he took his role as leader of the family ranching business. Although maybe now that he was with Pilar, he'd ease up. Maybe.

And Josh... Josh wasn't getting out of prison for another six months, right around when the baby was due. That would be quite the welcome-home surprise.

From there, the news would spread throughout all Cabrillo. People she'd known since she was in diapers would be whispering about Liliana Merrill having a baby out of wedlock.

The rodeo circuit would be ablaze with it as well. Getting knocked up by a bull rider would do wonders for her reputation, which was already on shaky ground.

Lil pushed out a gusty sigh. No, she definitely didn't want to tell her family just yet. She had some more wallowing to do. She'd made her bed and she was going to lie in it, but she wanted to flail about in the sheets a while longer.

Bea set her hands on her hips. "Aren't you on the pill?"

That was the biggest joke of all. "I am. And we used condoms. That's like a..." Lil calculated in her head. "Like a less than one hundredth percent of a chance." She pinched her thumb and forefinger together, held them up. "Like, this big of a chance."

Bea shrugged, clearly unimpressed. "Well, it can happen."

"Why did it have to happen to me?" Even Lil was kind of disgusted with how pathetic she sounded. But getting all that wallowing out also felt kind of good.

"Well, you could keep wailing." Bea rolled her eyes to let Lil know what she thought of that plan. "Or you could do something about it." She slapped Lil's phone into her hand, a rectangle of heavy chill. "You could call him."

Lil stared at the phone, the screen black, half of her face reflected in it. God, she looked sad.

Call him. She'd flirted with the idea since Vegas but hadn't actually done it. Normally she wasn't a bit shy with men. But Adriano... she was irrationally afraid of any rejection from him. He'd been the most intense sexual partner of her life—she didn't want to find out she'd only ever been an okay fling to him.

What would he even say when she told him the news?

A terrible thought occurred to her. "What if I just don't tell him?"

"What?" Even Bea—modern, single, feminist Bea—was shocked.

"I mean, the baby's going to be with me most of the time anyway, I don't need his money to support us, and he probably doesn't want a baby in the first place. I'd be saving us both a lot of grief."

It made so much sense. And sounded horribly wrong.

Bea just stared.

"Okay," Lil allowed. "Not letting the baby knows its father is wrong."

Bea raised an eyebrow.

"Okay, really wrong. But—"

Bea raised the other eyebrow.

"I was only thinking out loud." Lil tightened her grip on the phone. She'd been hoping out loud, really. The easiest thing would be for Adriano to simply say that he didn't want to be a dad and good luck in the future. The baby was complication enough. She didn't need a man in the picture.

But she did have to at least tell him.

"I don't know what to say," Lil admitted. Did you simply blurt it out or did you lead with some small talk first? Maybe something about the weather before segueing into *"Hey, guess what? It's also about to start raining babies!"*

Bea crouched beside her, patting her arm. "It will all be okay. People love babies."

Her cousin didn't do consoling naturally, but at least she was trying. She was one of the Spencer cousins, and that branch of the family always had been reserved.

As for Lil, she'd always been told she was Aunt Franny come again. Wild, rambunctious—a pistol.

Lil was going to be a mother now. Wild and rambunctious were no longer on the menu.

"I'm not ready for this." And she really wasn't. Telling Adriano, her family—hell, *having a baby*—she needed more time. To adjust, to do... something.

"Ready or not, it's happening."

Bea was right. No more time to wallow. Time for action.

Lil stiffened her spine, called up her contacts on the phone. "Okay."

And sat there, staring at the screen.

She had to tell him, yes, but what happened after she told him?

Please make this easy. Just ask to see the baby during the summer or something. Or not at all.

That one would be hard to explain to her future child, but better than trying to co-parent with someone who might not even be living in the States in a few years.

"What are you going to say?" Bea asked.

Lil wished Bea would simply tell her exactly what to say. Could you outsource a pregnancy announcement? Or was that bad form, especially when you were announcing it to the father?

"Well, I might go with 'Hi, been thinking about you. Oh yeah, by the way, I'm having your baby.'"

Bea shook her head. "Well, at least I know you're feeling better if you're making jokes."

"It's either that or cry." And she wasn't a crier. "I guess I'd better make this call."

She brought up Adriano's number, put the phone to her ear, and steadied herself for the most nerve-racking few minutes of her life.

"Hello?"

As his voice, so deep, so rich, hit her ear after all this time, her stomach dropped and her heart kicked, every nerve in her body going on high alert.

And she realized this call was going to be much, much worse than she'd thought.

Chapter 2

ADRIANO SILVA WRIGGLED HIS FINGERS within his glove, testing his grip on the rope once more. Wriggled and tightened again. Mentally checked the pressure in his palm and knuckle joints, comparing against the memory of other rides. Yep, nice and secure.

He punched down his own fingers with his free hand, his forearm bared by his rolled-up sleeve, the muscles straining beneath his skin. Not quite there. He punched his fist again. There. There it was.

He looped the free end of the rope back over again. Time to check his seat.

The bull beneath him jumped sideways in the chute, pinning Adriano's leg against the fence. Adriano ignored the pain, concentrated on keeping the bull quiet until that chute swung open.

"Easy. Easy, King Snake," the flank man called to the bull.

The bull settled again, but the tension... the tension flowing between him and Adriano was thick, electric. Adriano set his free hand on the gate, lifted and set himself down. No, too much to the right. Again, he reseated himself. Just a hair too far back.

He heard the gate man's short exhale of impatience and ignored it. Adriano would take exactly the time he needed to make certain he was properly situated for this ride. Not one second more and not one second less.

He tried once more. *There.* There was where he wanted to be.

It was time.

One last check of his hat—couldn't lose that—then Adriano gave a sharp nod to the gate man. The gate swung open...

And they were out, over a thousand pounds of angry bull charging out of the chute, Adriano clinging to its back.

Immediate snap left, Adriano only half a moment behind the bull. Arm high, chin tucked.

Snap right now, but Adriano was with him. Spur forward and back, forward and back.

More, a little more. He needed this bull to give him more if he was going to score high enough to final.

A high kick, the bull's back legs rising higher than Adriano's head. Spur forward, spur back. *Hang on.*

More of that please. And please God, let me stay on.

The bull went into a slow spin, kicking high with each revolution. *Yes, yes.* The bull did his best to slingshot Adriano off while Adriano did his best to hang on.

Hang on. Arm up. Spur forward. Spur back. Keep right on him.

A grunt left Adriano's throat every time the bull landed, the toll of hanging on needing some kind of release.

The horn. The horn was blowing. Adriano slipped his hand free and dismounted, the bull still twisting with rage.

Adriano landed in the dirt on his feet, his head spinning

at the sudden lack of movement. He went for the fence even before he could form a thought. He had to get clear, let the bullfighters do their work.

But King Snake was done for the day, loping out of the arena like a man leaving work when the whistle blew.

It was over. Adriano had survived, injury-free. A smile grabbed hold of his mouth even as his heart continued to pound. It had been a good ride. Better than good.

The crowd agreed—they were cheering, on their feet and screaming. He took a deep breath, the adrenaline beginning to ebb, and waved his thanks. It was always nice to have an appreciative crowd.

Shorty, one of the bullfighters, jogged over to him and handed Adriano his rope, slapping his back as he did. "Hell of a ride."

It had been. Now to see if the judges agreed.

"Ho," the announcer boomed, "we've got the judge's results right here—eighty-three! That puts Adriano safely in the final round."

The announcer's excitement echoed Adriano's own. He punched the air as the crowd roared its approval.

He could hit some good money here—if he kept it together for the short go. Another win and he'd rise one, maybe two more slots in the overall rankings.

If things kept on as they were—and they would—he'd finish in the top ten this year. Next year he'd take home the championship.

That had been his plan from the moment he'd stepped off the plane two years ago. He'd seen America break better riders than him—the money and the fame were heady drugs. But it wouldn't break him. He was ready for it.

The fame he could do without, but the money... for a

poor kid from Brazil, the money was insane. And the more he made, the more he wanted to make.

Not for himself, but for all the family he'd left behind: his mother, his brothers and sisters, his nieces and nephews. The more he made, the better he could make their lives.

Especially his mother's life. She deserved her last years to be comfortable ones.

He only prayed he could make it back home in time to spend her last years with her.

Next year, if he took the championship, he'd have more than enough money to return and set up his own ranch. That was his mantra these years in exile: *a few years more, a few dollars more.* It kept him going when the homesickness was at its worst.

Adriano looped his rope over his shoulder and left the arena, walking past the pens with waiting bulls, down a grim cinder block hall toward the locker room, his chaps smacking his legs with each step. He loosened his protective vest, shrugged out of it, welcoming the freedom from its weight.

His heart slowed and the triumph fled with the adrenaline, leaving him feeling hollow. That was always how it happened—eight seconds of a great ride, a few minutes more of the crowd's appreciation... but then there was the next ride, just around the corner, waiting for him. Always that next ride.

A few years more, a few dollars more.

But now only one year more if he kept his focus, stuck to his plan. And a lot more dollars.

He walked into the locker room and into a more muted celebration. The other bull riders shook his hand, slapped his back, and then turned back to their own waiting, focusing on their own next ride.

Adriano made his way over to his fellow Brazilians, about ten men huddled together in a corner, all wearing a typical cowboy posture—heads bent, hats shading their eyes, thumbs hooked into their belt loops, speaking together in muted Portuguese. They were in the same boat he was, riding here in the States to make a better life for those back home. The Brazilian riders stuck together since no one else understood what being the outsiders in the American rodeo circuit was like.

"Hey, Silva."

Adriano gritted his teeth, came to a halt. He put on a false, slightly dim smile and turned to face Colby Crane.

While the American and Brazilian riders mostly kept to themselves, there was a friendliness between them. At least most of them. But not Crane.

The American rider was tall and blond with a pearly-white smile in a square jaw—a poster-perfect cowboy. He certainly had all the buckle bunnies falling over him, even though his smile always looked like it was wrapped in barbed wire. At least to Adriano.

Crane had given Adriano the nickname of "Slick Eddie" back when Adriano had first joined the circuit. Adriano had explained that "Eddie" wasn't his name, and when Crane had continued to call him that, he'd realized: the point hadn't been to give Adriano a nickname. The point had been to piss Adriano off.

So Adriano tried very hard not to let Crane piss him off.

"Crane," Adriano drawled back, playing up his accent.

"Kind of funny you'd do so well riding a bull named Snake, huh?" Crane didn't laugh, but his smile stretched, showing his teeth.

Adriano got the implication but kept his expression blank, questioning. He shrugged, shook his head. "Okay." As if he didn't understand what Crane had said and was repeating the only English he knew. And he wouldn't make the mistake of asking Crane what he'd meant.

Crane's smile sagged. Adriano shrugged again—*you won't bait me, no matter how hard you try*—and turned back to his countrymen. The circle opened enough to let him in.

"You're right to ignore him," Miguel Barros said in Portuguese. Barros had been on the circuit longer than any of the other Brazilians and acted as a mentor. Most of them spent their time off at his Texas ranch if they couldn't make it back home.

Adriano took a breath, forced his limbs to be loose, and told his heart to settle down. "He was only trying to rile me."

He had to be focused on his next ride. No matter how it galled him to pretend he didn't understand, when he'd rather shove Colby's teeth down his throat than shrug it off. But beating the shit out of Crane wouldn't earn him any money. This next go-round could.

"He's only jealous," Miguel went on. "He wishes he could ride half so well."

If he trained as hard as I do, he might.

Playing with the buckle bunnies as often as Colby did came with a price—late nights and late mornings. Less time to train. When Adriano slept with women—and he did; he wasn't a monk, and being a bull rider had benefits beyond the money—it was only for the evening. Come morning, the lady was always gone and he was up just as early as the day before, training just as hard.

Besides, he couldn't fall for an American girl, not when he intended to return to Brazil. Only one woman had ever tempted him to go beyond a night together, but she'd made it clear that their interlude was only that—a fleeting moment that had ended.

He might think on her, a sliver of regret piercing his heart as he did, but she wasn't part of his plan. Riding the best bulls in the world, making as much money as he could while he did, that was his goal. His temporary American dream.

"It's not luck," Adriano grumbled. "I work hard. Harder than he does."

"I know," Miguel said, his gaze kindly. "It was quite a ride. You ready for the next one?"

"Yep." Grim, determined. Nothing would distract him.

"Best of luck then."

Adriano nodded his thanks and went to his gear bag, squatting down to set his vest, rope, and gloves inside. He rose, rolled his sleeve back down, and began to undo the buckles of his chaps, keeping every motion slow, deliberate, in order to clear his mind and calm his heart.

He stripped off his chaps, folding and laying them in his gear bag, then straightened.

The bag at his feet began to vibrate. His phone.

He shouldn't answer. Not in the middle of the locker room.

Unless it was one of his family members calling from Brazil. They were the only ones who usually called. Perhaps something had happened to his mother.

He rooted in the bag for his phone. It buzzed in his hand, the screen flashing a number he didn't recognize.

Not Brazil. Not about his mother then, thank God.

But who?

"Hello?"

A beat of silence in which his heart slowed.

"Hey, Adriano?"

His heart picked up again—he knew that voice. "Yes, it's me."

He stepped out into the hallway, keeping his head bent so that no one could see his expression.

"It's Liliana." Hesitant. Almost afraid. "Liliana Merrill."

He released a breath. *Liliana.* It really was her.

The one woman who'd tempted him to forget the plan and fall hard.

He'd wanted so badly to call her since Vegas. Never had a woman haunted his fantasies like she did. But what would he tell her? *Come meet me?* He had no apartment, no place of his own. He lived in hotel rooms. And it had been clear from the beginning—their fling was just that. Quick and hot and meant to end when they left Vegas.

But there had been many a night alone in his hotel room that he'd wished for her in his arms. Or in the shower. Or bent over a desk.

He shook those fantasies loose. "Hey, Liliana." He kept his voice low, level.

Maybe she was in town. Maybe that's why she was calling. Another fantasy tried to slip back in, but he pushed it away.

"Um, how have you been?" Her voice was too cheery, edging toward unnaturalness.

He frowned. With the hesitancy and the unnaturalness, something was wrong. She wasn't calling because she was in town. So what was it? "Okay. How have you been?"

"Fine," she said too quickly. "Actually... you remember Vegas? The National Finals Rodeo?"

How could he forget? The intensity of those days with her was like nothing he'd ever experienced before. "Yes." His voice lowered. "I do."

A short, small inhale from her, buzzing across the line. So she remembered too. "Well..." There was a scuffling in the background, as if someone was in the room with her.

"Look, there's no great way to say this." Defiant and strong, a definite turn from her earlier tone. "I'm pregnant."

The world fell away, the hallway, the noise from the crowd, the smell of dirt and cattle, the harsh fluorescent lights—all gone. Just him and that truth.

He was going to be a father.

He'd never known his father. Not truly. Adriano and his siblings had grown up in Mato Grosso do Sul on the ranch where his mother was a housekeeper. His father had worked in the state capital of Campo Grande, coming home only a few weeks a year. He'd died when Adriano was eight, leaving Adriano as the man of the family.

Adriano remembered strong arms, a wide smile. Occasional letters or pictures sent to them. That was all. Nothing more.

He'd never known his father as a son should. And he'd always felt the loss.

That wouldn't be his child's fate.

But I must go back home. He sagged against the wall, cold and rough against his back. This more than upended his plan—it blew it to bits.

The baby had to come with him. Lil was independent, headstrong. Perhaps she didn't want the child?

"You're keeping the pregnancy." He'd meant it to be more of a question, but he wanted her to say yes so badly it came out closer to a statement.

"Yes." With that word, she locked the both of them into... *something.*

"I'll be on the next flight," he said. Just as defiant and strong as she'd been. He could come up with a new plan on the flight. One that still had him returning to Brazil next year—only with his child as well.

"Whoa, wait." Her panic trilled across the line. "I didn't want you to... Where are you?"

"Texas." What did it matter where he was? Even if he were in Antarctica, he'd still come. This was *his child.*

She released a long slow breath, as if he'd said something crazy. "You don't need to come all that way. Maybe we can discuss some of this over the phone. Like how involved you want to be in the baby's life and such."

The placating tone set his nerves on edge. And her bit about how involved he wanted to be made his teeth grind together. "Do you really want to discuss the future of our child over the phone?"

She made a noise of exasperation, one that rasped along his ear. "No, but the baby isn't due for another six months. I don't need you here right this second. There's nothing to do."

He'd liked her independence in Vegas—he'd never had to worry that she'd form an attachment to him or what they'd shared. In a lover, he'd appreciated such independence.

But in the mother of his future child, he liked it less. "Don't argue."

She actually gasped. He didn't care—they'd start as he meant to go on.

"Look, if you want to do this in person, let's meet at your place," she said.

"I don't have a place. Not here in the States." Another wrinkle to consider. What was to be done with the baby during his last year here? Something else to consider on the flight over.

"Oh," she said. In that one syllable, he could hear her disapproval. "I guess we could meet here."

She'd been eager enough to meet him in Vegas, but her

invitation to her home territory was decidedly reluctant. Perhaps having a *Pardo*—part Black, part Native, part Portuguese, a pinch of everything that made up Brazil—with nothing permanent in his life as the father of her child wasn't something she wanted advertised. But if she was keeping the baby, he wouldn't be shoved into the shadows.

"I'll be there tomorrow," he said, anger making his jaw tight. "And we'll figure things out."

Silence on the line. He waited it out. She could offer all the excuses she wanted to—he'd still catch the next flight. Nothing was coming between him and this child.

"Do you need me to get you at the airport?" Grudging, but it was still a victory.

He smiled but kept it from his voice. "No, I'll rent a car."

"How will you know how to get here?"

"Your family owns a very large ranch in a very small town," he said, dry as the Texas town he was stuck in. "I'll find it."

He ended the call before she could say anything else.

He let his hand fall to his side, still clutching the phone. The coldness of the wall at his back had begun to seep through his skin, tightening his muscles, but he stayed in place. The discomfort was real. Real enough to anchor him just now.

A father. He was going to be a father.

That seemed completely *un*real.

Other riders on the circuit had children. Most of them had left behind wives and kids in Brazil, but Miguel Barros's kids lived here, on his ranch in Texas. They hardly spoke Portuguese, and Brazil was simply a place their father dragged them to a few weeks a year, during summer break.

They didn't appreciate the green of the Cerrado—a green that didn't exist here—vibrant, jewel bright. The grasslands with the gray, short-horned cattle making their way across them, wider than a man's imagination. Or the glittering emerald waterways of the Pantanal, the sunsets painting them orange and red. And the animals—macaws, monkeys, even the powerful jaguar—no, nothing like that here.

Sometimes he felt as if the sounds, the scents, the colors, the rhythms of that place, that life, were tattooed on his very bones. And his bones ached at being away from them.

Adriano set his fist to his chest, a surge of homesickness turning his lungs to stone. Miguel's children didn't feel this when they thought of Mato Grosso do Sul. Brazil wasn't home to them—only a boring trip that tore them away from their friends and life in America, a place to be endured until they could return home.

If Adriano's child grew up here, she might be the same. She'd never truly understand what it meant to be Brazilian ——the beauty, the richness, the joy of it. He couldn't let that happen.

And his mother... the kidney disease might take her tomorrow or two years from now. He couldn't steal his mother's chance to know this grandchild.

The baby had to go to Brazil. There was no other way. He'd seen some American child-sharing agreements— almost the entire year with the mother while the father got the summers. Two months. He needed more than two months. Two months a year was nothing in a child's life.

Perhaps Lil would be open to the inverse of that. Most of year with him and the summers with her. Perhaps.

He rubbed a thumb across his chin. He'd have to see how much convincing it would take to get her to agree to that. And in the meantime, he'd care for her, protect her—

show her how well he'd watch over their child once it was here.

No lawyers though, that was certain. He didn't want to involve any lawyers. The Merrills could afford to hire a team of sharks to savage him in court—and a foreigner, trying to steal a child from its American mother? Oh yes, he knew how the courts would rule on that.

No lawyers, no judges. Only him, convincing Lil that his plan for the baby was best.

She was headstrong, independent. She'd give him a fight if she didn't immediately agree to his plan.

He put on a grim smile. She could fight all she wanted. He rode bulls for a living—he was certain he could tame one stubborn woman. Even one as stubborn as Liliana Merrill.

Chapter 3

THANK GOD FOR PILAR.

A fervent prayer on Lil's part, because this meeting would have been much, much worse without Pilar's calming influence. Pilar's sweet tones could soothe the beast—the beast being Lil's older brother, Benedict. That was probably why Benedict was going to marry Pilar one day.

The three of them, along with her other brother, Luke, were sitting in Benedict's office in the resort, the one from which he ran the family enterprise. An enterprise encompassing one of the largest ranches in southern California and a luxury resort. Lil might run the stock operations and Luke the hotel, but Benedict ran all of it.

He wasn't running anything now. He sat behind his desk, staring worriedly at her while Pilar hovered over his shoulder. Luke had propped himself against a wall, arms crossed, his forehead knit with concern. Lil sat across from Benedict, feeling like she'd been called into the principal's office.

Just tell him. The longer you wait, the more freaked out he's going to get.

But she couldn't quite find her voice.

"Lil has something important to tell you," Pilar prompted, setting her hand on Benedict's forearm.

"I know that," he growled. Not that Benedict was mean, but he carried a lot of responsibility, so he tended to leave off the pleasantries. "So what is it?"

Her tongue sat flat and numb against her clenched teeth.

When she'd called her parents—just after Adriano had insisted on coming and then hung up on her, the jerk— they'd been cautiously happy. Although she had heard her mother whoop in triumph before she'd hung up the phone.

Lil hadn't been too worried about her parents, not really. They loved her and all her siblings, loved them fiercely, but they'd always expected their children to be independent, to bear the fruit of their own decisions—sweet or rotten.

So they'd be happy grandparents and leave all the fretfulness off since it was Lil's burden to bear. Besides, Lil was bringing into the world a new Merrill, a new generation to carry on their traditions. That was always a happy thing.

She wasn't too worried about Luke's reaction either. He'd huff and puff and threaten to blow Adriano's house down—which didn't even exist; yet another headache—but Luke would come around in the end. Look at how she'd convinced him to go ghost hunting in the barn loft when they were kids, or to play white-water rescue in the creek. Or the time they'd decided to climb as high as they could up the old oak, trying to touch a cloud. Luke still had the scars from that one and loved telling the story—especially to an interested lady.

Yeah, Luke would come around. But Benedict... He was old-fashioned. He had ideas about how people should behave—how his siblings should behave most of all.

When Josh was convicted, Benedict hadn't budged an

inch in his anger. Having a baby out of wedlock wasn't even close to nearly killing your girlfriend in a drunken wreck as Josh had done—but it still wasn't Benedict's idea of how people should behave.

Hell, for all that he and Pilar made googly eyes at each other, they hadn't moved in together. Waiting for a white wedding and all that.

Liliana wasn't getting a white wedding. Not that she'd ever wanted one.

She blew out a breath. Right. Time to confess.

"Remember when I was at the NFR a few months ago?"

"Yes." Drawn out, as if Benedict was trying to sense where she was going.

"There was a man there."

Benedict's ears went red. "I probably don't want to hear the rest of this, do I?"

No more than she wanted to say it to him. But it was too late to shut the barn door—the horse was already loose.

"Probably not." Her voice caught as her cheeks heated. "I uh…" *Ah, hell. Just say it.* "I'm pregnant."

Benedict's ears went from red to bone white, along with the rest of his face. "What?"

There it was. His older brother's about-to-open-a-can-of-whoop-ass voice.

Luke pushed off from the wall, his fists clenching, and let out… a growl. He honest to God growled.

Lil's stomach twisted—and not from morning sickness. But she'd admitted it. Now it was all over but the shouting.

Pilar patted Benedict's arm. "You know where babies come from, dear."

Benedict's frown eased and he laughed. Actually laughed.

Thank God for Pilar. The knot in Lil's stomach slipped loose.

Luke's frown changed into something closer to resignation, although he didn't laugh. But Lil knew that look of his. It would be okay.

"I know you're upset," Lil began.

"Yes." Gruff, rather than harsh, from Benedict.

"I know you're disappointed." Best to get that one right out in the open.

He frowned again. "Disappointed? No. I only want to make sure you and the baby have everything you need."

"We're here for you, Lil." Luke had dropped his arms and his tough-guy act. "Always. Whatever you need."

She rubbed at her nose. She knew her brothers loved her, but sometimes when she got new proof of it like this, it could make her teary. She cleared her throat. "Thanks guys. We'll be fine."

Benedict actually smiled. "We've always got your back. Even if we wish this had happened a little differently."

"Me too." She shrugged. "But it is what it is now."

"Did you tell Mom and Dad yet?" Luke asked.

"Yeah. I think the promise of grandkids outweighed any disappointment. Josh..." Josh was a tricky subject around Benedict. But he was still their brother. "I'll tell Josh when I visit him next."

The trip north to see Josh in prison was a long one, and she couldn't just drop in whenever she wanted. Telling him over the phone seemed a little cold, but maybe it would come to that.

Luke blew out a wry breath. "I'm gonna be an uncle. Another little Merrill running around." The ends of his mouth tipped up. "He's gonna get into all the same shit we did. And he'll be a steer wrestler."

"The hell he will," Benedict said. "He'll be a roper."

Lil rolled her eyes. "And maybe she'll do whatever she wants and not have her uncles push her into stuff." But she was smiling. The baby wasn't even here, and the family was already welcoming him or her with open arms.

"She can run the bull-breeding operation once she gets old enough," Benedict offered.

If the bucking-bull project was still viable by then. But Lil wasn't getting into that just now.

And speaking of bulls... they'd never asked about the father.

Pilar wanted to though. Lil could see the question pushing at her lips.

"So you guys are probably wondering about the father," Lil got out with fake enthusiasm.

Benedict snapped back into being a disapproving older brother, and Luke slipped into the role of tough guy.

"Who is he?" Luke demanded, clearly wanting to know so he could send a fist into the guy's face. Great.

"He's not from here," she hedged. "I don't know if you guys have met him."

Benedict raised an eyebrow. "He doesn't live in Cabrillo?"

How much had Benedict heard of the "Tiger Eyes" story? Hopefully not much. "No. I actually met him in Vegas."

A deep inhale from Benedict told her that the picture was becoming clearer. He knew the kind of men she liked to *hang out* with there. "Do I know him?" The older-brother warning tone was back.

"You definitely know *of* him." She put some fake sunni-ness into her voice. Here it was. "He's Adriano Silva."

Benedict's jaw began to clench. "Yeah, I've heard of him."

"Motherfucker," Luke breathed.

Okay, so they had heard of him. Probably not good things. Although, *she'd* never heard anything particularly bad about Adriano, only the typical bull rider's stories, and she was closer to the circuit than her brothers.

"Does he know?" Benedict asked.

"I talked to him last night." Hearing his voice yesterday had made her heart flutter. And the rest of her too. The velvet rasp in his voice had proven that he remembered her fondly. Remembered and perhaps hoped for more. But probably not the *more* she'd given him.

After that, his voice had been all firm command. Adriano was going to force himself into the picture, whether she wanted him there or no.

He was the baby's father, so probably best not to think of it as *forcing*. But it had felt like that.

When he'd said that he didn't have a place here in the US—not even an apartment—panic had flared in her. Because if he hadn't put down roots here, he might be planning to return to Brazil.

One more thing to discuss with him.

Benedict was shaking his head. "You shouldn't have done that. Let the lawyer talk to him first."

"Yeah," Luke put in. "You don't need this guy. You've got money, you've got us—you don't need him. Or to deal with him if you don't want to. Let the lawyers work everything out—custody, visitation. You don't need the stress of face-to-face stuff. Not with a baby on the way."

Benedict was nodding along while Pilar looked mildly worried.

Lil nibbled on her lip. It would make things so much easier to let the lawyers handle everything. Especially after his surprising insistence that he come out right away. One call to the family attorney and she'd have a safe distance between her and Adriano Silva. A comfortable distance.

But she'd just had to make things harder on herself. Not to mention that it would be wrong.

"It's okay," she said. "There's no need for lawyers yet. We'll discuss it like rational adults and come up with a plan. I doubt he wants to raise a kid by himself. He's coming out today, and once he sees this place, he'll agree staying with me is best for the baby," she said with only half-faked assurance.

She'd wanted to meet with him somewhere else, or better yet, hash it out over the phone so that when she told her family everything would have already been settled. She could have said, *See? We've already got it all worked out.* Instead, she was fumbling before them like an idiot. And now she'd have to work out everything with Adriano under their noses. *Blech.*

"What do you want, Liliana?" Pilar asked gently. "Not what your brothers insist on, not what you think you should want... What do you really want?"

Good question. Too bad she didn't have an answer. "I'm not sure. He seemed very committed on the phone." Too committed for her comfort. Too demanding. She was only just getting used to the idea of having a baby. Adding a man into the mix... Well, she needed a little more time. Not that she was going to get it.

"Whatever you decide," Benedict said with firm conviction, "we'll support you."

Pilar nodded, the both of them wearing expressions of steady support and concern.

Luke's expression was about the same, but with a hint of grudging sheepishness. "Me too. But if you want him gone, only say the word."

Her throat started to close, so she went round the desk to hug Benedict as tightly as she could. He could be crabby and stern and play *I'm the eldest, hear me grump* a lot, but he was first and foremost her big brother. And she loved him for it.

Then to Luke for an even tighter hug and quick pat on her back. God, she loved the both of them. And the baby would love them too. So, so much.

A final hug with Pilar, and then Lil was sitting back down, wiping at her eyes. "Thanks guys. Really, it means..." Her throat closed too tight for her to finish that.

"Of course." Benedict nodded, his expression going grim. "When your—" His mouth twisted as he searched for the right word. "When *he* gets here, send him to talk with me when you're done."

Great. So much for Benedict taking it well. She tilted her head, blew away the last of the tears. "Benedict, don't do anything crazy. I can handle this on my own."

"I don't do crazy," he said. "It'll only be a little chat with me and Luke."

Pilar raised her eyebrows behind Benedict, as if to say *Fat chance.*

Luke pulled up a shit-eating grin.

Lil groaned. Benedict and Luke double-teaming the poor guy? Adriano might have been too pushy on the phone, but he didn't deserve that. "Benedict, I know why nobody would date me in high school. Please don't do this."

"Nobody would date you in high school because all the boys were scared of you. You were tougher than they were, and you never took any shit."

True. And not taking any shit definitely made it hard to date. Not that she'd ever been really interested in relationships.

"It's going to be hard to work things out like adults if he thinks my family are assholes."

Luke laughed. "Good. Let him think we're assholes as long as it keeps him scared."

"I only want to feel him out," Benedict said. Pilar gave him a look, one he could see this time. "And let him know that Luke and I are looking out for you," he confessed.

Ha. As if their *talk* would be that innocuous. "I think Adriano will figure that out on his own." A couple of glares from her brothers would get the point across right quick.

She sighed. Whatever. If Adriano couldn't handle a talk with her brothers, maybe he shouldn't be too involved in the baby's life. Because she and the baby and her family were going to be a package deal. *Love the baby, love my brothers.*

Her phone buzzed. She fished it out of her back pocket, her heart stepping double time when she read the message.

"He's here." Breathless and giddy as a girl getting asked out to prom. She took a deep breath. *Steady. Be chill.*

Time to go hammer out exactly what kind of a co-parenting relationship she and Adriano Silva would have.

He was waiting for her in the front courtyard, his back to her as he studied the fountain there. From this angle, he looked pretty much like any cowboy. White straw Stetson, dark blue button-down shirt, crisply ironed Wranglers, battered and dusty gear bag slung across his back.

His hat covered his close-cropped dark curls, but the line of his neck was exposed, dark skin glowing golden in late-morning sun.

"Hey," she called out.

He turned and her heart stopped. This, this was where he differed from the average cowboy. Deep bronze skin stretched tight over high cheekbones, his jawline razor sharp. And his eyes... lighter than his skin, they glowed like chunks of the finest amber.

Yes, he would be a perfect match for *Style Magazine* with those looks.

He studied her for a long moment, his gaze so intense she would have sworn the temperature rose ten degrees. "Hey. How are you?"

Jesus, she'd forgotten how devastating his accent could be. The syllables seemed to slide around his tongue. It just wasn't the same hearing it over the phone—it didn't hit her right in her belly. And other places.

"I'm good." She shoved her hands into her back pockets, rocked on her heels. She'd known it would be awkward, but this lust mixed with self-consciousness made for excruciating awkwardness. "Thanks for coming."

"No problem." But his voice went tight, as if it *were* a problem.

She gestured to the resort behind her. "I got reservations for lunch. So we can talk."

He tipped his hat back, studied the resort with narrowed eyes as if the thing was a personal affront to him.

She'd seen that look before, the one that said, *You don't deserve all this, spoiled princess.* Her teeth ground together. Yes, her family had money. Lots of it. But she worked as hard as anyone else. Nobody could say that she didn't get her hands dirty in her job. All that money would come in handy when she was raising their child.

"All right," he drawled. "Let's go."

She led him through the hotel to the steak house, thankful that no one would think it strange she was having lunch with a random dude. She entertained clients of the stock operation all the time—everyone would simply think Adriano was one of them. They could figure out he was the father of her baby later when she was more mentally prepared to handle the stares.

The table in the private room in the steak house was already set when they arrived; Hank, the waiter, was ready to take their order.

Adriano's expression remained grim as he helped her into her chair. This was going to be super fun if he kept that attitude up. Too bad she couldn't sip some liquid courage while she did this—but no more liquor for her for another several months.

"What'll you have?" Hank asked, all brisk professionalism in spite of the fact that Adriano continued to scowl at her.

"The seared ahi salad," Lil said without looking at the menu. "And a coffee, thanks."

"Tuna?" Adriano asked. As if *tuna* were some kind of supervillain.

She stared at him. "Uh, yeah."

"The book says no tuna." He said *book* as if it were the Bible and *no tuna* was the first commandment.

"Why can't I have ahi?" She loved the stuff. Yeah, it was kind of expensive, but it wasn't like she was dripping furs and jewels. She wore button-downs and jeans and battered ropers, same as everyone else. She could have some damn ahi for lunch.

"Too much mercury. It will ruin the baby's brain."

Her mouth fell open. "It will *what*?"

Hank took a step toward the door. "I'll just come back in a few minutes."

"No," Adriano said. "I'll have the steak frites. She needs something high in protein and iron. And folic acid. But no fried food."

Hank nodded. "I can put something together that fits that." He practically ran toward the door.

And now he knew she was pregnant. Awesome. This was already just awesome.

She stared at Adriano. "How did you know I needed to eat all that?"

He stiffened, the lines of his neck going stark. "Just because I'm a bull rider doesn't mean I'm stupid."

She gentled her tone. "I never meant that. *I* didn't even know I needed all that."

He bent down, rummaged in his gear bag. "This is what you need to read. I picked it up before my flight left, read it on the plane."

She took it. *Your Best Pregnancy: How to Maximize Your Baby's Potential Before Birth.* It was actually bigger than a Bible, nearly a thousand pages. "Wow."

"Yes." He tapped the cover. "There's an entire chapter on things you should not be eating. And another five chapters on all the things you should not be doing."

A whole book on what she couldn't do. How wonderful.

"You can keep that copy," he offered. "I'll get another one for myself."

She blinked. "You bought an entire book on things I shouldn't be doing?" *Control freak.* She did not want a control freak watching her every move. Or her child's.

"I've never dealt with a pregnant woman before. I wanted to be prepared."

Wait, how much dealing was he planning on doing with her?

His gaze intensified. "How are you?" His voice was low, urgent. "Have you had any sickness?" His grim expression had dissolved into worry. Pretty serious worry.

"No, I'm fine," she assured him. Concern was sweet.

Concern was nice. She could work with that. "So fine that I didn't suspect anything was wrong until a few days ago." It was kind of stupid to not realize you were pregnant until three months in, but she'd been fine, still been getting her period up until last month… not even gaining any weight. She understood those women on the "I Never Knew I Was Pregnant!" shows a little better now.

If she hadn't finally missed her period, she might have never known. Until the baby took a good kick at her liver.

His mouth twitched at the word *wrong*. "Have you seen the doctor? Does he think everything is fine?"

"The doctor is a woman, and I'll see her tomorrow." Guilt moved in her—but she *hadn't known.* If she had, she'd have been to the doctor long before now. She wasn't neglectful.

"I'm coming with you." Oh, the command was back in his tone. As if she'd suggested he couldn't come and he was slapping her down.

Her own mouth twitched. "I never said you couldn't." Although she wasn't enthusiastic about it. But he was the father. "We can get you a room at the hotel if you like." Which brought up another sticky situation. "So, you don't have a place of your own?"

"No. It didn't seem necessary—" His jaw tightened. "I didn't need a place here since I always planned to return to Brazil."

There it was. She released a slow breath. Okay. Okay, they could still make this work. Somehow. "I take it you're still planning on doing that?" She was proud of how steady her voice was.

"Yes." Quiet and solemn. "Although my main plan is to support the baby as best I can."

She shifted in her chair. "Good." Time to tackle the

biggest hurdle. "When would you like to have visitation? Maybe during the summer? Do you even want visitation?"

Please say no. Make this easy for both of us.

"Your summer is our winter," he pointed out. As blandly as if they weren't discussing their child's future. "And I wasn't thinking about something like visitation."

"Oh? What then?" Maybe he was simply going to waive all his parental duties.

"I propose that we marry and that you and the baby come back to Brazil with me."

She choked on her next inhale. "Marry?" *No.* "I hardly know you. I'm not going to marry you. And as for leaving—I can't leave Cabrillo. My family, my job, my entire life is here." Her pulse hammered in her throat, as hard as if her heart had actually jumped up there.

"Your job? But once the baby is here, you won't be working any longer."

Her temper ignited. "Excuse you? Of course I'm going to keep working." Even if the bull breeding failed, there was still the stock operations. She had to pass that on to this baby. "I don't think you understand how important my job is."

"What does the doctor say?" He was infuriatingly cool.

She stumbled on that. "I... I haven't asked." Of course she wouldn't do any of the really dangerous stuff anymore, but the rest should be fine. Right?

"Hmm." He drummed his fingers on the table. "Let me see if I understand. You mean to keep the baby. You mean to keep working. Which means while the baby is with you, someone else will be caring for it most of the time. And you're willing to offer"—he cocked an eyebrow—"summers for me? Do I have it right?"

He did, but he didn't sound pleased. Not a bit. "What, do

you want the entire year and me to have summers?" She laughed in disbelief.

He didn't. "Yes. Why not? This year I will finish in the top ten. Next year, I win the championship. And then I return home, ready to enjoy my retirement."

That was... very detailed. She frowned. "You can want to do those things, but that doesn't mean they'll happen. No one can plan for that." But looking into the deep glow of his golden eyes, she wasn't so sure.

"Watch me."

Oh boy. This was a lot more determination than she'd been expecting to be up against. "And who'll watch the baby while you're riding? A nanny?"

"Yes."

"So it's okay for you to use a nanny but not me?" Infuriating. Absolutely infuriating.

"Only for a year. You'd have the baby with the nanny always." As if she meant to hand the baby over to some stranger and just forget about the kid.

"I don't think you understand." She *knew* he didn't understand. "This baby has a legacy to inherit." She gestured to everything around them—the resort, the ranch, the entire mountain valley. "Our family has been here for over a century. We've had the ranch just as long. That's what Merrills do—they run this ranch. My child can't grow up not knowing that legacy."

"And you think that our child doesn't have a legacy in Brazil? No grandmother, no aunts, uncles, cousins, waiting there? That there isn't an entire country, a culture, that's also her legacy? One that she'll never truly know, not in only two months out of the year. To say nothing of her father." A muscle in his jaw clenched. "Not to mention that my mother is ill. Our child might only have a few years to get to know her. Or should I say two months out of a few years. Why is it automatically right that the baby be with you most of the time and not with me?"

Because I'm the mother. Emotionally it was the only answer. Logically it wasn't an answer at all. Because he was right—why should Lil simply assume she'd get the baby most of the time?

Because I just should.

"I'm very sorry about your mother," she said.

Something flickered deep in his gaze—pain? No, she couldn't let that sidetrack her. It was sad, but that didn't mean she had to hand the baby over to him.

"I'm very sorry," she tried again, because she was, "but I still think the baby should live with me."

"And yet you give no compelling reason why."

Because she just should.

She shook her head. This wasn't working. Only five minutes into this and they'd already stumbled into a massive knot. She pressed a fist into her belly, trying to push away the sourness there. "Maybe we should each get a lawyer. Work things out that way."

A retreat, but one she needed. He couldn't take her baby away from her, away from the family who already loved the child.

But he had a point—the baby had another family in Brazil. One that probably would love the baby as much as the Merrills.

"No." His eyes widened for half a moment in what looked like panic, then he went back to being stone faced. "No lawyers."

"You don't know anything about babies." Perhaps not the greatest counterargument, but it was all she had. But she'd never imagined he'd want to raise the baby on his own.

"Neither do you."

"I don't... Look, I don't know what to think." She ignored his scowl. That was more than fair, for her to be confused about all this. She'd only just found out she was pregnant. "We had a weekend together—an amazing weekend—but that was all. And now we're having a baby. But we hardly know each other. You want to get to married or have me simply hand the baby over to you..." She gestured futilely. "I just don't know."

"What can I do to convince you?" As coolly said as if this were only a business deal.

"Maybe I need to convince you." Yes, that was exactly what she needed to do. The gears whirred in her brain. "Why don't you stay here for a while, see the ranch, the history here—my family's history—see the kind of life I can give the baby, then decide?"

Oh yes, that was how she would do this. She'd prove that the baby being with her was best. That he'd be robbing the baby of a terrible opportunity if it lived with him. The baby would be part of a massive ranch, a family legacy that spanned over a century—who would turn that down for their child once they really understood it?

He leaned back, his mouth tightening as if he were holding in a smile, and she had the terrible impression she'd stumbled into a trap. "And perhaps I need to convince you. That I'd be a wonderful father to our child and the best thing would be for me to have the baby in Brazil most of the time. No nannies, no day care—with me, once I retire from the rodeo."

Aw, hell, it *was* a trap. Or at least a very dangerous bargain.

Best to tread carefully here and spell out exactly what they were proposing. "So I try to convince you the baby should stay with me most of the time? And you're trying to convince me of the opposite?"

He nodded. "Once the baby is here, we decide who was the better convincer."

She blew out a long breath. It was cold—but was a custody arrangement hammered out through lawyers any worse? "And if we don't come to an agreement by then?"

His gaze shuttered. "Then we bring in the lawyers."

She didn't want to do that any more than he did. Because if the lawyers got involved and they went to court, that offer of his to raise the baby without a nanny was going to look very good for his case.

She only had to make certain that she won their bargain. Easy as pie. "How do you plan to convince me you're the better option?"

"Well, I can't take you back to Brazil and show you what our child would be missing if he or she stayed with you. So I'm going to take care of you. Proper care of you." His voice was like velvet, dark and softly rough. Any other woman probably would have melted to hear him say in that voice that he wanted to take care of her.

Too bad for him she wasn't into being taken care of.

She had the feeling he was calling a bluff she hadn't even known she'd made. Or that she was wandering into yet another sticky situation with him.

Or perhaps he was bluffing, with all the *getting to know you* and *wanting to take care of you.* They were both probing for weak spots here.

If he was bluffing, she ought to call it.

She looked him square in the eye and laid out her hand.

"Since you don't have a place of your own and you want to *take proper care of me*, why don't you just move in with me?"

SHE WAS as audacious as ever.

Adriano stared back, knowing she was throwing out a dare with that last suggestion. The spark in her eyes, the jut of her jaw—she was begging for a reaction from him.

He hadn't expected her to say yes to his marriage proposal. That had only been a spur to see which way she bucked.

But look where he'd steered her to in the end.

He wanted to smile, but that wouldn't be taken well. Living together—yes, he could show her exactly the kind of father he'd be then. She'd realize that he was right, that the baby would have a better life with him, and he'd win. He always won when he put his mind to it.

Living together brought up the question of sleeping together though.

No. No, they should not be sleeping together. Not that she was offering it. He had to stay focused through this entire ride with her, just as he would a bull. And when he was focused, there was nobody better.

When he wasn't focused though... He'd been so distracted by her news last night he'd been thrown in the final round. Any more *distractions* from her and this year would be a complete bust. He'd simply have to learn to keep thoughts of her and the baby away when he was competing. Having more memories of her naked and wrapped around him wouldn't help with that.

But Lord, when Liliana had come walking toward him,

all long legs and fierce stride, his body had kicked into high gear, his every instinct screaming at her nearness.

With her fall of dark brown hair swinging in time with her step, she'd looked much as she had in Vegas—determined green-gray eyes the color of the ocean at dawn and skin that was kissed by the sun every day. She'd strode across that convention hall toward him, and he could only stare as she'd stalked him—and he hadn't been able to look away from her for the next three days.

If there was ever a woman who demanded a man's attention, it was Liliana Merrill.

She'd been at the NFR as the head of her family's stock operations, and he'd been there to ride bulls. When they hadn't been doing what they were supposed to, they'd been naked, sweaty, and entwined.

The more he'd had of her, the more he wanted. And she'd felt the same way. When they'd parted that last day, the regret had been almost more than he could handle. But there was no place in his life for a woman. Not even one like Liliana.

Even if he was going to be living with her.

"I'm guessing you don't have a little apartment you rent somewhere in town," he said, sarcasm biting in the words.

She colored just a hair but didn't deny it.

He glanced around the room. He didn't want to stay here, on her family's territory. He'd known the Merrills were rich—you couldn't be in the rodeo world and not know that. But Adriano hadn't quite known how rich. It made his skin itch to know that no matter how much he earned on his own, it would never match what Liliana had earned simply by being born.

Adriano was proud of being a *peão*, a country boy. But

having that pride rubbing up against wealth like this for months on end... he didn't like it.

The entire resort was done in what they called mission style. There had been places like this in Brazil, old places from the time of Portuguese rule, built by his African ancestors. Not fakes like this.

There were many families on the circuit who bragged about how they'd been ranching for over a century. But this place... this place practically intoned, *We've been here for several centuries. And we'll be here for many more.* It was a place that made a kid who'd grown up in the kind of poverty these Americans couldn't imagine feel as out of place as a bull in a milking shed.

"No," she said. "I live in the ranch house. With my brother Luke."

"Ah. So I move in and we all become one big happy family?"

She chewed on that, her soft lips pursing as she did. He didn't remember her kisses as being soft though. They'd been as fiercely demanding as the lady herself.

"Luke will come around," she said finally.

Adriano wouldn't put money on that. But she was the pregnant woman here, and if he wanted to turn her toward his plans, he'd have to give in to some of her demands. "If you're certain."

That caught her by surprise. "Are you saying yes?"

"Yes. But we'll have to set some rules."

"No sex," she said quickly.

He smiled at how rapidly she got that out. He didn't even have to steer her into that one. "I agree."

She pointed a finger at him. "And we'll have to agree to compromise on stuff."

"Like we've just been doing?"

She laughed, clear and strong and uninhibited. It hit him right in the chest, made his mouth tip into a wide smile of its own. Her laugh was a powerful thing.

The waiter came back then with steak frites for Adriano and a spinach Cobb salad for Lil. "Here you are," he said cheerfully, as if he hadn't backed away from their argument earlier. But once their plates were down, he was out the door again quick as could be.

Adriano dug into his steak. It was excellent, perfectly cooked and with a rich flavor he didn't get often in the beef here.

She was eating her salad fairly steadily. Good.

"Make certain to eat all that," he said. There, there was a bit of care.

She rolled her eyes. "This isn't going to work if you're going to order me around."

He blinked in surprise—that had hardly been an order. "I only want you and the baby to be safe. This won't work if you're going to be headstrong."

"Welcome to Headstrong City, cowboy. If you want to convince me, you better be ready to meet me halfway."

He almost laughed but kept his expression still. He didn't want her to think she could get around him with humor, no matter how powerful her laugh was. "I'm here, aren't I? This is your territory."

That hit—he could tell by how her eyes widened, just a fraction. "I don't exactly own all this. It's owned by the company, which benefits the entire family."

Ah yes, that legacy she'd been going on and on about. As if she was the only one who cared about family. "You said Luke lives in the ranch house. What about the rest of the family?"

She smiled as if amused by a private joke. "Oh, don't

worry. You'll get to meet them. Soon. Benedict and Luke want to have a chat with you."

Damn. He'd only just arrived, and already her brothers were throwing their weight around. Although to be fair, he'd have done the same if it were his sister.

"And where can I find them?"

Her smile went smug. If she weren't pregnant, he'd kiss that smile right off her face. And she'd kiss him back just as powerfully, and soon enough there'd be dishes flying.

He blew out a low, slow breath, trying not to let her hear. Moving in with her was going to be hazardous to his self-control. *Focus.*

"Benedict's office is off the main corridor," she said. "Follow the signs pointing to the corporate office."

Corporate office. As if he were an employee to be repri-manded. "Sounds easy enough."

She was laughing again, but only with her eyes. "Oh, it is. And be sure to tell Luke and Benedict I said hi."

She thought they'd scare him. He was a bull rider—two angry brothers weren't going to run him off.

"Of course." He let his own smile grow smug, watched her expression sag into uncertainty. "I'd be happy to."

Let her think she'd won this battle. He was only setting himself up for the longer struggle to come.

One he was prepared to win.

Chapter 4

OH, THESE TWO THOUGHT THEY were tough.

Adriano lounged in a chair across from Benedict Merrill's desk. The man himself sat behind it, another man propped against the wall behind him.

The office itself was stark, luxuriously bare as only the truly wealthy can achieve. All eyes were meant to be on Merrill, not some decorations. Funnily enough, his secretary had enough plants out there to start a nursery. She'd also given Adriano a small smile as he'd walked past, so he wasn't entirely surrounded by enemies.

Benedict hadn't risen when he'd entered, hadn't offered a chair, hadn't said anything more than, "So, you're Silva?"

The other man said nothing, simply leaned against the wall with his arms crossed. His sleeves were rolled up to the elbow, revealing tattoos twining down his forearms and ending at the wrist. Adriano knew his type. Tough enough to cover himself in tattoos but still made certain they'd never show beneath a suit.

Adriano had no tattoos. His scars from his rides were

mark enough of his character. No need to set it in black and white, not when it was already carved in relief.

"That's me," he agreed. He slowly jiggled his foot as it rested across his knee. Enough to speak to impatience but not anxiousness. "You must be Merrill." He flicked a glance to the other brother. "Both of them."

Neither were pleased at his casual manner, he could tell. Well, he wasn't pleased at this show of force.

"Liliana's a Merrill too," Benedict said. Staking his claim on her.

"She's carrying my child." Adriano had a claim to stake as well. "That makes her part of my family now."

The silent one didn't like that. He shifted, the ropes of muscle on his forearms bulging. But he couldn't deny it.

That one must be Luke, his new roommate. Her other brother. Oh, Adriano had a surprise coming for these two.

Benedict folded his hands together. "How exactly did that happen?"

He damn well knew, but he wanted to Adriano to recite it like a shamed teenager.

"The same way these things always happen." They'd used protection, but... Well, God had willed it. "If you think I mean to shirk my duties to Liliana, you're wrong. We're moving in together."

"What the hell?" That got the silent brother sputtering, his movements jerky as he shoved off the wall.

Now who had control of this little meeting? Adriano sat back, putting on a half smile.

Benedict motioned for silence. "Moving in together?" He watched Adriano closely, his body quiet. If he was pissed, he was hiding it well. "That strikes me as... extreme. Liliana agreed to this?"

"She did." Let them think it was his suggestion.

Benedict's jaw clenched—he was struggling with this. He clearly thought stepping up to take charge of a lady pregnant with one's child was the right thing—yet when the lady in question was his sister, he liked it less. "We're standing by Liliana in this. No matter what she decides."

If she were to decide that Adriano had to go, they'd be quicker to throw him out than they were to welcome him, he could tell.

"I am standing by Liliana as well. And *our* child."

Luke snorted. "Great. So I'm supposed to live with her *and* you?"

"Yep. I'm guessing the house is big enough that we can avoid each other." Adriano didn't keep the sarcasm from his voice. He wasn't cowed by their wealth. Or even impressed.

Benedict drummed his fingers on the desk. "Huh. You don't have a place of your own?"

"There's no need. I'm always traveling for the rodeo." Nothing to be ashamed of in that.

Benedict leaned back, his gaze sharpening, keenly speculative. "Look, I get it. You grew up poor, have no place of your own."

Adriano doubted very much that Benedict understood him. Not if he called this place home.

"You find out Lil is pregnant," her brother went on, "and you think this is your chance. A place to live, all her wealth—"

Fuck you. "You think I grew up in a *favela*?" Always the *favela* with these Americans, as if his home held nothing else. "How would I have learned to ride bulls in a city? Brazil is more than beaches and *favelas* and *Carnaval*. I grew up in Mato Grosso do Sul, nothing like the beach or Rio de Janeiro. Not that you've probably even heard of it." *Small-minded idiots.* "I came to this country to ride bulls, not seduce rich girls. And I make good money riding bulls." He jabbed a finger at Benedict, his teeth snapping together. "I've no need of Liliana's wealth. If you're not convinced, take a look at my lifetime earnings on the Internet sometime."

Adriano might not be rich enough for these fools, but he was rich enough for this country. And coming from where he had, that was saying something.

"I already did," Benedict said mildly. "And I investigated what your sponsors are paying you. I'm not saying it's nothing, what you've earned, but some men can never have enough. And Liliana has a lot. Enough that even a man as rich as you are might covet it."

Adriano could understand the impulse to protect his sister, but he wouldn't let that come at the expense of his honor. "I went to Liliana because I was compelled by her. Not her money." Something flickered in Benedict's gaze. "It was her own self that drew me. You insult her to suggest differently."

She still compelled him, that brash attitude coupled with her delicious body, no matter what rules they'd laid down. And she was to be the mother of his child, always and forever. Benedict could sling all the slurs he wanted and it wouldn't undo that simple fact.

No matter that Adriano meant to convince her to give their child to him—he'd still defend her.

"That's a pretty speech." Benedict made it sound anything but pretty. "But words ain't shit. You've got to prove they're true. I guess if you're moving in with Lil, you've got the chance."

He didn't need to earn Benedict Merrill's approval—he was his own man. And yet, he *was* Lil's brother.

You'll have to meet me halfway.

Well he was about to, not that she was here to see it.

"The baby will want for nothing. I swear it." Not quite a concession, but perhaps better than one.

Benedict put on a rather cruel smile. "And I'm just in the pool house, in case you two need anything."

Lil hadn't mentioned that wrinkle. One brother in the house, one next door—how many more relatives were going to pop out of the bushes, promising to watch over her?

Adriano smiled back. "Wonderful. That will make Lil happy—and we all want her to be happy, don't we?"

The brothers had no response except for matching scowls.

LILIANA PLUCKED AT A WEED, imagining that it was Adriano.

Not that he was scraggly, green, or unwanted. No, he was as irresistible as he'd been in Vegas. His eyes still looked too beautiful to be true. And his skin, several shades darker than his eyes, the color of antique gold or aged bronze. The luster of it put her in mind of velvet, but under her fingers it had been as smooth and warm as slept-in sheets. And beneath his shirt and Wranglers, a body that could have been a Greek statue come to life.

She sighed. God, listen to her. Going on about him like some overwrought poet. He did that to her though. Made her lose her head and wallow in her visceral response to him.

Rufio, her Jack Russell terrier, set his paws on the edge of the raised garden bed and cocked his head as if to say *Are you okay?* One of the barn cats watched from the fence, silently judging them.

She rubbed the dog behind the ears. "Letting him move in might be a terrible mistake."

It felt good to admit that aloud, that everything might go to hell. Adriano's behavior over lunch had been worrisome.

Yet... he'd bought that pregnancy book. And read the entire thing. It was kind of sweet—except it was probably all part of his plan to convince her he should have the baby.

Some might say she shouldn't have suggested moving in together so quickly, should have taken her time, gone slow.

But that had never been Lil's way. She always had to make things harder for herself. Perhaps if she'd gone slower in Vegas with him, this might not have happened. But it was done now. The only way out was through.

Assuming he survived his meeting with her brothers.

Lil found another weed and pulled it from the soil. A little weeding each and every day kept the garden neat. And it soothed her, looking over her plants, smelling the sharp scent of their leaves and the deeper notes of the soil beneath, getting the dirt on her hands. These had been her mother's garden boxes before her—Lil could still remember her father mortaring the bricks into place, the excitement of keeping the secret until her mother's birthday.

Rufio tore off toward the house, barking at something coming along the path on the far side. She chuckled at the sight. He was so little, yet so fierce, all of him jerking with the force of his barking. His tail began to wag and his barks turned from menacing to friendly.

Lil rose and brushed the dirt from her hands, knowing who was coming.

Her brothers appeared, looking grim.

No need to ask how their meeting with Adriano went. Maybe they wouldn't be moving in together after all. But she suspected it would take a hell of a lot more than her brothers' anger to run off Adriano at this point.

"Hey, Lil," Luke called.

Benedict simply nodded.

"Hey, guys," she said. The look on Benedict's face just killed her. He hadn't looked like that since Josh had gone to prison. "How was your day?" she asked brightly, as if none of this pregnancy stuff had ever happened.

Luke stared at her for a moment, then cupped his forehead in his palm and started laughing. "Jesus, Lil."

But Benedict remained grim. Always the worried older brother with him.

"Okay," she said, "tell me this: is Adriano still alive?"

Luke laughed harder while Benedict kept on frowning.

"Of course he's alive," Benedict said.

"Oh good. That would have been hard to explain to the baby."

Benedict did smile then, but only for a moment before the scowl was back. "Are you certain about this?"

Hell no. "It's too late to turn back. You guys didn't scare him off, did you?" She kept her tone light, airy, as if her stomach weren't tying itself into knots.

"If he's not scared of you, then he ain't going to be scared by us." Benedict said it with grudging admiration. Apparently Adriano had held his own with her brothers.

"I can't believe you're letting him move in here. But you want him gone, tell us and he's gone." Oh so easy for Luke to say that. As if he could toss Adriano out the front door, dust off his hands, and the matter would be settled.

If only it could be that easy. But Adriano's insistence that he was just as fit a parent as she complicated things, along with the situation with his mom. Not to mention their bargain, which she definitely was not mentioning to her brothers.

"We're trying it out while we work on the visitation stuff." The truth, if an airbrushed version of it.

"And if it doesn't work out?" Benedict raised his eyebrows, the all-knowing older brother.

She didn't want to think of that. It would be like being divorced, only without having ever been married. The two of them might be passing the kid back and forth like a game of hot potato.

Not for her baby, not if she could help it. But she couldn't deny Adriano's wish to return to Brazil, to his family—and to have his child know his homeland too.

"It has to," she said. "You got your he-man chest-thumping talk with him, and now you two need to keep out of it." She'd never convince Adriano that Cabrillo was the best place for the baby if her brothers continued to piss him off.

"It doesn't *have* to work out," Luke said, crossing his arms.

Oh Jesus. "Knock it off. It was cute before, but now that he's here, you've got to cool it." If Luke screwed this up for her...

She pushed past them and went for the house. Rufio followed, stumpy tail wagging.

"Where are you going?" Benedict demanded. "We need to talk about this more."

She kept on. "I have to finish dinner. Which he's coming to, so best behavior please." She stopped, turned back. "Benedict, are you eating with us?"

"Yep." Residual anger made the edges of his voice ragged. "Pilar is coming too, if that's all right."

"Of course. I *actually* like Pilar."

Benedict rolled his eyes. "Okay, fine. When shit goes south, you deal with him yourself. Go right ahead."

Lil gritted her teeth. "Maybe I will." She would call him on his dare. Just watch her.

She turned—and stopped dead when she saw Adriano. His hat shaded his eyes, but the set of his mouth was grim—and he was holding a huge bunch of roses.

"Oh. Hey." Weak, but she wasn't expecting him to be listening in on her fight with her brothers. *Great show of family unity there.*

Rufio jumped up on him, leaving dusty paw prints on his Wranglers.

"Down!" The dog was usually better about that, but it seemed that her entire family was out to embarrass her today.

Adriano smiled as he rubbed at Rufio's ears. "It's okay. He's happy to see me." He straightened and his mouth flattened again, probably because she wasn't as happy as her dog was to see him. He shoved the roses at her. "How are you? Did you rest today?"

"I'm fine, and no, I didn't rest today. I'm not a kindergartener." Not even five seconds here and he was already starting in. But the roses were nice. Almost *date-like.*

Adriano frowned. "But you're pregnant."

"She knows that," Benedict barked.

She sighed. "Let's go in," she said to Adriano. Dinner was going to be just wonderful, with these men being so charming and polite and all. Thank God Pilar would be there. They could take their plates to the kitchen and let the men duke it out in the dining room.

"See you at supper," Luke called in a voice that dripped insincerity.

She grabbed Adriano's arm. "Come inside and see the

house." The house was sure to impress him—any kid would be happy growing up in a house like that.

The muscle beneath her hand was steely taut, his body almost close enough to brush against hers. The roses were tucked into her other arm, as if she were a prom queen leading her king to the stage. But she was leading him into her house. Which was now his house. Or his temporary house at least. The surrealism of the scene wasn't lost on her.

She opened the back door, letting Rufio go ahead of her. Once they were in the kitchen, she dropped Adriano's arm but kept hold of the roses. She wasn't much for roses—too water-hungry for California—but these were a deep burgundy so dark as to be almost black. There were only five, and the blooms were already blowsily spreading their petals, without the pinched secrecy of a bud. Where had he managed to find these?

As she arranged the roses in a vase, she watched him from the corner of her eye while he removed his hat and took in the kitchen. She could finally see his eyes, gleaming amber in the late afternoon light. His mouth was flat, much as it had been when he was looking around the resort.

She fiddled with the roses, whose scent was suddenly overpowering, and waited for him to speak. Most people oohed and aahed when they saw her kitchen, or at least said something vaguely polite about it. But his mouth stayed firmly shut.

He walked slowly to the window, his boot heels echoing against the tile, a *thunk, thunk, thunk* against her ears. She dragged her fingers against the petals of the blooms, causing a few to fall to the counter. Was he ever going to say anything?

After several moments of staring out the window, his

mouth finally tipped up in a smile. But his eyes remained sad. Or maybe resigned. "Is that your garden?" As if he already knew the answer.

She wasn't quite expecting that. "Yeah. It's a hobby of mine."

He half turned to her, the sunlight sliding across the plane of his cheek, lightening his skin to the color of a new penny. "More than a hobby, as big as it is. My mother had a garden like this. I haven't seen it in many years."

Her heartstrings twanged. To be away from home for years must be so wrenching. No wonder he was eager to return. And he'd said *had*—perhaps his mother was too ill to garden any longer. Lil swallowed. "That was my mother's garden before it was mine. So the baby will get a green thumb from both sides of the family." It was an attempt to lighten the mood, but the loneliness cloaking him remained. "Thank you for the flowers," she finished quietly. "You shouldn't have."

"You're the mother of my child."

Wasn't that romantic? Not that they were in this for the romance. No matter how hot she still found him or how sad his expression made her.

She grabbed the vase, a few more petals falling as she did, and set it on the dining room table, taking a minute to breathe. Just a minute, just to get steady again. This wasn't about romance or attraction or anything that had been between them before—it was only about the baby. And who got to raise it.

Back in the kitchen, she avoided his gaze. She opened the oven and checked on the gratin, which bubbled and popped. "Supper's almost ready."

"What is that? It smells delicious." He sounded surprised, as if she shouldn't be able to cook.

Don't let it get to you. He'd change his tune once he tasted it. "Oh, a spring veggie gratin I thought I'd try. Mainly an excuse to use up some of the stuff that's in season."

A child would eat well in her kitchen. He'd see.

Luke came in then, slamming the door a little too hard, his boots ringing a little too loud. No doubt he thought they were up to something and wanted to warn them he was coming. No need for him to worry though—they had a no-sex clause in their all-about-the-baby bargain.

"Smells good," Luke said. "And I got your bread. Are you sure you don't want to come work in the hotel kitchen?"

"Ha." She poked him with a wooden spoon. "As if I'd ever leave the stockyards and be stuck in a hot kitchen all day. Not to mention having to take orders from you."

Luke grinned. "You'd be a terrible employee too. What do you want me to do?"

"Do?" Adriano seemed puzzled by that.

"Yeah," Luke said with an edge. "Do to help fix supper."

"You can set the table," she said hastily as Adriano's face darkened.

"What can *I* do?" he asked, like a bull lowering its head for the charge.

God, if they started fighting about *helping* her...

"Luke, go set the table. Can you get a bowl down from that cabinet?" she asked Adriano. She pointed hard at the cabinet, trying to distract him. "It's for the salad." Luke gave her half a second of a shit-eating grin, then disappeared into the dining room.

She snapped her fingers. "Oh, and I've got to start the chops. Do you like lamb?"

"Who doesn't like lamb?" Adriano was stretching up to reach the salad bowl, back arched, butt flexed, and her heart jumped.

Jesus. "You, uh, you'd be surprised." Her mouth was suddenly too dry. "But I'll take that as a yes." *Breathe.*

She crouched down to the cabinet by the stove and pulled out a cast-iron pan—only to have it snatched from her hand.

"Hey!" She spun around to grab it back from him.

He danced—actually *danced*—out of reach. How did his hips do *that*?

"That's too heavy." His accent had thickened, his vowels going sinuous, the consonants twisting off his tongue. "You're not supposed to be lifting heavy things."

And here they went again. She narrowed her eyes. "I hauled hay this afternoon and each bale weighs about a hundred pounds more than that pan." Her arms hadn't withered to nothing the moment he'd knocked her up.

He set the pan on the stove, wearing an expression she could only call *supreme jackass.* "Well, you can't haul hay anymore either."

As if that just decided things. "You can't order me around." This was already turning into a colossal mistake, and he hadn't even moved in yet.

"Ask the doctor tomorrow. She'll agree with me. It's all in the book."

She wanted to burn that stupid book. "I'll definitely ask her. And she'll say it's fine. Women have been having babies for ages and never stopped doing their chores. My great-great-grandma Cat had five babies and probably never once took an afternoon nap. Didn't have the time."

Let him argue with that. She came from hearty, fertile stock. None of this pregnant princess for her.

"You're not your grandmother." Not even a slip of the *supreme jackass* face. "And you were not this argumentative in Vegas."

They'd hardly talked in Vegas. Not that it had always been sex. They'd slept quite a bit too, just holding each other. And when she was awake, she found she couldn't stop touching him. Every inch of him was new and addictive, her fingertips yearning to know, to touch, all of him. She'd spent hours being held by him, touching him with her hands, lips, limbs. He'd done the same to her.

Well, no wonder it had been different: he hadn't been this much of an asshole then.

"We're not in Vegas," she said shortly, her skin feeling too tight. She turned back to the stove, poured a slug of oil in the pan. Cooking. Cooking was good; cooking was calming. She lit the burner, ignoring the father of her child at her back, and when the oil went thin and hot, she set the chops in. The oil spit back at her.

"Whoa." Adriano wrapped his hands around her waist and pulled her away from the stove.

She pulled away from him, trying to outrun the sensations he'd set off. *He's trying to restrain you, not seduce you.* "Hey! I have to sear those. You're supposed to keep the baby away from the stove, not me."

If that stupid book said she couldn't cook any longer, she was burning it for sure. She'd get into Luke's fireworks stash and set that thing off in a blaze of glory.

Adriano held on tight, forcing her to turn around in the circle of his arms.

Well, that wasn't much better. Now they were face-to-face, her hands on his chest, his arms wrapped around her back, their mouths inches apart. Way too close. Her heart raced and her clit went heavy. Great. *Thank you so much for being on my side here, vagina.*

She pushed against his chest, tried to wriggle out of his grip. But that made it worse, so much worse.

He didn't even budge, keeping his back between her and the stove, his arms tight around her. And his pelvis hard against hers. "Tell me what to do and I'll do it."

Fuck me hard enough to make my teeth rattle.

No, better not say that. Wouldn't want to violate the no-sex clause.

"Fine." She pushed again and this time he let go. "But you better do it right. My brothers won't be happy having their chops ruined." Or coming in on their sister being manhandled in the kitchen.

"Neither will I." He went for the tongs, totally unruffled. And that answered the question of whether he was still attracted to her or not.

"No." She set her hand over his before he could grab the tongs.

And forgot what she'd been about to say. How did he have such hot skin? Or maybe her skin was superheating. Tension radiated from his arm, down through his fingers, zapped hers, and ran straight up her arm to her brain.

His eyes met hers and all the oxygen left the room, ignited by what was between them.

Their bodies remembered, wanted, yearned. Hers did at least, and judging by the dark gold of his eyes, his did too.

Hell, her body more than remembered—she wanted to devour him, to explode with him again and again until there was nothing left but sated exhaustion, just as they'd done before.

"Adriano?" She meant *Do you feel it too, do you want this as badly as I do, until you can't breathe, can't taste anything but your lips on mine?*

"Liliana." Deep and low, a growl with a touch of force. Yes, he remembered. And he wanted.

Thank God she wasn't alone in this. She put a hand to

his cheek, felt the sting of stubble there for half a moment, then captured his mouth.

Oh yes. This, this was what she'd needed all these months, the pressure and taste of him on her mouth, his heat caressing her. He made a noise that vibrated along her lips and through her mouth, then pulled her close.

She parted her lips and there was his tongue—aggressive, demanding. She demanded right back, tangling her tongue with his and sliding her hand along his cheek and then to his neck, gripping tightly.

More. Now.

He obliged, his large hands finding her ass and gripping her as tightly as she was him, grinding his pelvis against hers.

Zero to sixty. That was how she liked it, and he gave it to her each and every time.

She rubbed against him, felt the hardness grow. Oh yes, he wanted it as much as she did, as fast as she did. She started to drag him backward toward the counter, where she could—

Something hot snapped at her forearm.

"Ow!" She jumped back from him, rubbing at the stinging spot.

Grease, from the pan. Her arm was rapidly developing livid spots from it—but the burns were small and didn't look that serious. Just another day in the kitchen.

Adriano seized her wrist, twisted her arm toward him, muttering under his breath in Portuguese. "You make me forget myself."

No, that hadn't been a forgetting. That had been a remembering.

She shouldn't have done that. She had to keep her head with him.

"Are you all right?" His voice was harsh, as if she were forcing him to ask her.

"I'm fine." She stepped back, put chill into her voice. "You don't need to turn the chops this early. Don't rush it."

He slid her a look that clearly said, *Take your own advice.*

She rubbed at her forearm, her desire curdling in her belly. He'd been kissing her as hard as she'd been kissing him. She hadn't been alone in her wanting—he was just as much at fault.

"Sear the chops until they're browned, then slip them into the oven for ten minutes." She backed toward the kitchen door, away from him and toward the safety of her brother. Adriano couldn't kiss her and reject her with Luke watching. "I think you can manage that. And look, you got me away from the stove." *Point: Adriano.*

She left before he could call her back.

Chapter 5

ADRIANO DROPPED HIS GEAR BAG and looked around the guest room—the room that was now to be his.

It had a TV and lace curtains and a floral bedspread and even a few bland china knickknacks on the dresser. It was a pleasant enough room, one that no one had ever made their own. A room that sat empty most of the time.

There had never been an empty room in the house he'd grown up in, with its dirt floors and lack of electricity.

Lil stood in the middle, wearing a hotel-manager smile. She'd been quiet at dinner—which had been amazingly good—leaving her brother's girlfriend to do most of the talking.

"It's very nice," he said, nice being as bland in English as it was in Portuguese. "Thank you." He could tell she wanted him to be impressed by the house, by the size of it, but if his childhood had taught him anything, it was that the size of the house didn't matter—it was the love contained within.

Lil's smile never slipped. "Good. Towels are in the bathroom. Let me know if you need anything else."

He wouldn't be surprised if she told him to call the front desk anytime, so impersonal was she.

She was pissed. He'd never thought she'd be the kind of woman to hide her anger like this, but that's what she was doing. No doubt she was holding back because of their bargain. He was certainly holding back because of it—but not anger.

"If that's all, I'll see you in the morning," she chirped. "Doctor's appointment is at ten. You can use Josh's truck if you need to." Her face darkened for half a moment.

He didn't want to drive a borrowed truck, but that could wait. "Who's Josh?"

Her expression held on to the darkness, went blacker. "My brother."

A brother who wasn't here and made her look like that. Not good. "Where is he? Why doesn't he need his truck?"

She pinched her lips as if holding in something bitter. "He's in prison. For a DUI."

Adriano didn't know much about the American legal system, but a few bull riders he knew had been caught drinking and driving—and they'd never been sent to prison. Her brother must have injured or killed someone.

"When is he getting out?" He wouldn't push on the issue of what had really happened. Upsetting her was bad for the baby. And her belly was too flat—he'd have to ask the doctor about that tomorrow.

Thank God he was here to take care of her.

"He's coming home just after the baby is due."

Coming home. Which meant that brother lived here as well. And that brother would be living with Adriano's child too, once he came home. Something to file away, in case he needed it for the court case.

"Are your parents coming soon?" he asked. Meeting

them was certain to be as unpleasant as meeting the brothers, but it must be done. The sooner the better. That was always the best way to get things done to his mind—do the worst and hardest first and the rest was all easy.

"Oh, I'm sure they'll come eventually. At some point." She seemed quite unconcerned. "They're retired and have their own thing going on in Cambria."

The welfare of their daughter should be *their thing*, but best to let it drop. Another point against Lil though—his mother would be close, since he planned to buy a ranch and move her to it. His mother wouldn't have her own *thing* going on.

Lil rubbed at her arm.

"How's your arm?"

She glanced at it. "Fine. When you cook you get burned."

Hardly convincing. He clasped her wrist to see for himself, gentler than he might have liked. But after that kiss in the kitchen, he needed to watch himself around her. She was like a lit match to the gasoline of his libido. He'd not win this bargain by seducing her. At least, he didn't want to win it that way. He tugged her toward him. "Let me see."

Her skin was warm and smooth, a much lighter shade of brown than his own. There was no mark there, only freckles left from the touch of the sun and tiny hairs finer than an angel's. His thumb rubbed against the bone of her wrist, her pulse leaping under the tips of his fingers.

"See?" Her voice was rough and low, edged with desire. "Just fine."

His gaze met hers. The color of her eyes was more gray than green, an ocean readying for a storm, her breath drawing quick and deep. Just as his was.

She leaned into him, her arm bending back as he held it.

Was she trying to break his hold? Or was she trying to get closer?

He wanted her to get closer, or at least his body did. But she ought to be breaking his hold.

She wasn't. Her gaze was steady on his, her body leaning into him, his fingers tight around her wrist.

This was wrong. There were reasons he should stop, reasons that had been so clear at lunch. But he couldn't remember them, could only remember those wild days and nights from before, the two of them locked together, sweat slick and climaxing as one. That was all he wanted—no focus, no bargains, only the two of them together like it had been.

He released her wrist, set his hand into the notch of her hip, fingers curling round the upper swell of her ass. Such a sweet ass it was too.

He sank his fingers deep, deep enough to have her gasping. "I gave you a bruise here," he said, as breathless and rough as her gasp had been. "That third day. Do you remember?"

A dark purple bloom to mark the ferocity of that night. He'd been absurdly proud to see it the next morning, his basest thoughts howling, *She's mine, see how I've marked her.* A dangerous impulse, given that there should have been nothing permanent between them.

"I remember." Lil's hand slipped between them, slid down to his upper thigh, squeezed hard. "I gave you a bruise too. Right here." Her fingers dug even deeper. Her other hand found his bicep, tested the muscle there. "And I bit you here."

He couldn't hold back his groan since he did remember, her mouth hard and mean and wet there as he thrust deep into her pussy, soft and sweet and wet.

He lowered his mouth to hers. Just one kiss, just to take the edge off. He could stop after one kiss. A kiss wasn't technically sex.

Her lips were silken, her tongue bold, her fingers painfully tight around his arm. He welcomed the ache, rolled his hips into it, because it proved how badly she wanted him, how deep her need for him went. Deep enough to dive toward pain.

His own fingers tightened on her hip, pulled her into him. The moan she gave vibrated down his own throat, so closely were their mouths joined.

Take her to the bed. Get those clothes off.

She was already unbuttoning his shirt, her hand slipping inside. Her fingers found one of his nipples and pinched.

He took her bottom lip gently between his teeth, a promise that he'd pay her back in kind for that. Just as soon as he got her shirt—

"No."

He tightened his grip on her hip.

"No." And she took a step back, her gaze clear, defiant.

That expression had set him aflame in Vegas. When she'd said she wanted him, wearing that expression, he knew she meant just that. She wanted *him*. Not because he was a bull rider, not because he'd be a notch in her belt. But simply because she wanted.

"We agreed," she reminded him. "And you forgot. This time."

A lesson then. Payback for his kiss in the kitchen.

His temper flared, but he damped it. Just barely. "We—"

She held up a hand, backed toward the door. "I know. *We shouldn't have.*"

"We couldn't even hold to that for a day." He was chiding her as much as himself.

"Actually, we did." She wrenched open the door. "We stopped. Or I stopped."

"This time." He could teach some lessons as well.

Lil snorted. "And the next time too."

His head jerked back. "There won't be a next time." He would keep his focus. He had to.

He always won when he kept his head—and he couldn't bear to lose his child.

Her fingers tightened on the doorknob. "Yep. It's all about the baby, right? And our *bargain*." Her tone was sharp enough to slice open a tin can.

Adriano couldn't argue with that. "Yep. What time is the appointment again?" Not quite as sharp as her tone, but sharp enough.

"Ten."

"Good."

"Good." She shut the door hard enough to let him know she was pissed, but not really a slam.

He sank down onto the bed, looked around at the room that was now his. His first night here and they'd already almost fallen into bed *and* gotten into an argument. So much for showing her how well he could care for her. Or their child.

If there was a worse omen for his victory here, he didn't want to see it.

THE NEXT MORNING, Lil set her forehead against the goat's flank, the coarse hair scratchy against her skin while the warm, musty smell of goat filled her nose. The milk went *hiss-hiss-hiss* against the stainless steel bucket as her fingers worked, milking in the pearl-gray light of dawn. The doe munched contentedly at her feed, happy enough to stand still.

Lil was content enough herself. Morning chores did that to her: milking the goats, feeding the chickens, checking the drip on the garden and the orchards, ensuring that her little slice of the ranch was running smoothly. After her coffee, she'd go to her office and ensure that the bigger slice of the ranch—the stock operations—was running smoothly as well.

Too bad her personal life was a tangled mess. They shouldn't be sleeping together, not at all. But damn it, she still wanted to. Her body recognized his in a way that seemed to go deeper than instinct.

She was reminded of something she'd heard during sex ed in high school: *Sex is for a night, but a baby is forever.*

It was meant to scare them into being responsible—or to not have sex at all—but it was true. She'd had Adriano for herself for three nights. And now she'd have his baby for the rest of her life.

If she kept her head, convinced him she was right, it could be her daughter doing this with her one day. Every day.

She sighed and burrowed her head a little deeper into the doe's side. The doe held steady, firm, a warm comfort on that morning.

Lil finished the milking, put the doe away, poured the milk into the pasteurizer, and cleaned out the bucket. She'd make cheese with this milk, she decided.

Rufio came bounding by as she left the milking barn, chasing after a crow that had dared to land too close. The crow cawed back at the dog and hopped into the nearest pepper tree, beak open wide as it silently laughed at the still-barking dog.

She took a deep breath of the chill morning air, needing this meditation of chores and livestock and cool gray skies before she started her workday. This had been her routine since she'd been seven, old enough to begin caring for the stock. And she still did it today. Just as her father had before her and his father before him.

The crunch of gravel came from behind her and she turned.

Adriano walked toward her, dressed much as she was—heavy work jacket, jeans, and boots. Only he was wearing a black Stetson, and she was bareheaded. God, but he looked good, hips swiveling, a dusting of stubble scattered across his high cheekbones and that blade of a jaw.

"Morning," he said softly. There wasn't much hesitation in him today—more like resignation.

"Morning," she said in return, mirroring him. She wasn't certain where to go in all this herself. It was too nice a morning for scrapping. And sniping at him was bad for her meditative state. "Want to help me collect eggs?"

He nodded and they headed off to the chicken coop. Her hens were happily pecking at the scraps of apple she'd given them earlier, hardly even noticing that she was stealing their eggs. The shells were brown and cool as she dug in the straw for them, handing them to Adriano to slip into his pockets.

"When I was young, this was one of my jobs on the ranch," he said, his accent thick. He did that when he talked about his home, let his English slip closer to his native tongue.

"Me too. My first one, actually."

They shared a smile.

"I can fry some of those up for you, if you like." She

latched the coop behind her. No need to mention that it could be their child collecting eggs from this very coop one day. He was smart—she could leave it unspoken and he'd still hear.

"And yourself?"

She started for the house. "Oh, I usually just have coffee."

He caught up to her, frowning. "Doesn't that have caffeine?"

Crap. "Can I not have *coffee*?" She'd never survive the next few months without coffee. It was inhuman to expect her to.

"The book says—"

She held up a hand. "Please God, not the book."

"The book says," he went on with a grim look, "that you should not have caffeine. And you have to eat regular meals. Preferably six small ones a day."

She'd be eating all day at that rate. There'd be no time for anything else. "How about this? I'll eat breakfast as long I can have some coffee with it. And that will be the only coffee I drink all day." She'd have a bitch of a headache come the afternoon, but it wouldn't hurt to cut back a bit.

He opened the door for her, still scowling. "We're not negotiating about this—you're definitely having breakfast. But I suppose one cup of coffee in the morning can't hurt."

Wow, how magnanimous of him. "Look at us. Our first compromise," she said dryly.

A smile played at the edge of his mouth. "Where do you want the eggs?" he asked.

"Just here on the counter. I'll cook them up for us."

"Will the cooking be dangerous like last night?"

She laughed. Oh, he was adorable like this. She'd never thought he could be. "No, it will be perfectly safe. How do like your eggs? Mine, I go for over easy, with some toast to mop up the yolk."

"But the book says—" He stopped at her look. "What I meant was, is it safe for you to have uncooked eggs?"

She was about to tell him *of course*, then caught herself. All these restrictions on pregnant women seemed so silly—but there were so many. What if there was something to some of them? And how did you decide which were the ones you ought to follow?

If she went by everything in Adriano's book, she wouldn't be able to get out of bed.

But eggs *were* kind of tricky. These were probably safer than commercial eggs—but they'd still come out of a chicken's butt.

Their kid would definitely be safe if he or she lived with him. No dangerous eggs on any of Adriano's plates.

"Let's scramble them," she decided. "And put some smoked salmon in. And little bit of..." She went to the fridge, rummaged in it. "Oh yeah, a little bit of this goat cheese. Add some toast and fruit and it's a completely balanced meal."

She motioned him away from the stove and set about cooking the eggs, putting some slices of bread into the toaster between stirs.

"What can I do?" he asked.

"Can you get some of the cherries from the bowl there and wash them?"

He went to work himself, the two of them settling into an easy silence. She poked at the eggs, checked their consistency. A few more seconds and they'd be ready. The toaster chimed. Perfect. It was all coming together.

Adriano was putting the cherries into a bowl, stealing

one as he did, his teeth flashing white as he tugged it from the stem. "Wow, these are good."

"Those are descended from trees my great-great-grandma cultivated. She developed that variety." Lil didn't bother to keep the pride from her voice. "Right here on this very ranch."

He stole another, leaving a smear of red across his bottom lip. She could clean that up with her tongue if they hadn't instituted that no-sex rule.

"Is this the ancestor who had no time to sleep?" A teasing note made the words rough.

"Yep." She didn't rise to the bait—Grandma Cat had been a tough lady, no matter what Mr. Adriano Silva thought. "Eggs are ready." She divided them between two plates and set the toast on the side.

She spooned some on her toast, took a bite. Mmm. That was good. She took a sip of coffee, black and strong. That was even better. She gave a happy sigh. There was nothing better than simple food well prepared.

Adriano raised his mug to her. "My compliments."

"Thank you." She took another big bite. Maybe she should eat breakfast more often. This was nice, having something filling to wash her coffee down with. Although she only got the one cup today. And for the next several months.

Before she could cry at that thought, she asked him, "What are you going to do this morning? I've got to work before the doctor's appointment." The question felt weird, like he was her kept man or something, but she didn't think he'd be happy rattling around the house, and he didn't seem the type to watch much TV.

"Is there a gym nearby?" He kept his eyes on his plate,

probably as embarrassed as she. "I ran this morning, but I'll need to find a weight room eventually."

He'd already run this morning? He must have woken up earlier than she had. "There's a gym next to the garage with weights and stuff. Luke uses it." Adriano's grimace told her what he thought about sharing a gym. "He won't mind if you use it though." If Luke did, she'd have a talk with him.

"Thank you." His grimace didn't quite die. "And thank you for the breakfast." That was more sincere.

She drained her cup of coffee—her last cup for the day—and nodded. "No problem."

Their gazes met—and the air between them ignited. Her heart began to pound, her skin tingling, and her mind only bent on closing the gap between them, pressing her mouth against his.

No. Hell, she was in deep trouble here if only looking at him could send her off like this. Speaking of sending off...

She backed toward the door. "I've got to go. Just leave your plate in the sink"—her back met the edge of the counter and she gave a little grunt—"and I'll see you back here in a few hours. I'm sure you can find the gym."

He watched as she backed away from him, silent, intent—which wasn't really helping matters.

Her fingers found the knob, wrenched the door open. "Later."

She practically ran out the door but couldn't quite escape the desire still pulsing through her blood.

Chapter 6

THE DOCTOR'S WAITING ROOM WAS WEIRD.

No, that wasn't quite right. It made Adriano *feel* weird, filled with women carrying huge bellies, beaming husbands next to them, rings glinting on their fingers. The couples all had their heads together, laughing about names and baby gear and what their babies would be like when they finally arrived.

Lil's belly was flat, her finger bare, and Adriano hadn't said more than two words to her the whole time, his mouth numb with unease. No happy cooing for them.

She flipped through the stack of paperwork she had to fill out, sighing as she did. The size of it made it look more like a novel than a medical history.

Her pen hovered over a question. "Are there any genetic diseases in your family?"

He blinked as if coming out of a bad dream. "What?"

"Genetic diseases: cystic fibrosis, Tay-Sachs, things like that."

How the hell would he know? This was an entirely different world, the diseases carrying strange names. Names a doctor had given them. Doctor's visits had been rare when he was growing up, reserved only for serious, life-threatening things.

His mother's illness had come on just after he'd left for the States, so his sisters had been the ones to navigate her through all those doctor's appointments. Although Adriano had paid for it. Once he was home, he would help more, as a proper son should. And hurry up the transplant if he could.

A few years more. A few dollars more.

But first, to get through this appointment. And prove to Lil that the child should be with him.

"I don't know about any of those diseases." He hadn't meant to sound so short, but his jaw wouldn't unclench. The soft music piping through the ceiling wasn't helping—it was just bland enough to be irritating.

"Okay. We'll mark *no* for that." Her pen scraped across the paper.

"My mother has kidney disease." He hadn't meant to say that, but he closed his mouth too late to trap the words there.

"Ah. Does she have to go for dialysis?" Lil got all soft when sympathy took over her expression. He liked it, seeing as how she was so rarely soft.

"Yes. My sisters take her." He paid for it, yes—but he could still be there, helping more.

"Can she get a transplant?"

"She's on the list, but..." He blinked. He mustn't tear up in the doctor's office. "Well, of course I want it to happen now. She will though. Soon enough."

All false assurance that. No matter how he tried, the deepest part of him was convinced he would return home too late.

Lil set her hand on his forearm. "I'm sure she'll get the

transplant in time."

But there was something in her gaze, something holding her back.

She thought he was manipulating her here.

He turned his gaze to the floor. This stupid bargain was tainting everything. He was being sincere, and she thought he was only being a cunning asshole.

"What else do you want to know?" he ground out.

"The next question is—Oh." She nibbled on the end of the pen, sent him a wary glance. "Is your father still living?"

Why would the doctor need to know that? "No."

She dropped the pen from her lips. "Oh. I'm so sorry. How did he die?"

Was this for the medical history? Or did *she* want to know?

"An industrial accident." Her gaze went limpid, sympathetic, urging him on. "He worked in the interior. I didn't see him much as I was growing up. I hardly knew him."

"I am sorry. I wish you could have known him." She made a note on the clipboard.

He clenched his fists around the arms of the chair. So it was just for the doctor then. He shouldn't have said that last bit; the doctor didn't need to know that. It made Adriano sound like some sad, penniless, foreign orphan, and he certainly wasn't that.

Her pen moved on the next question and stopped. "Um. It wants to know if we're living together."

"Of course we are." Hadn't they shared breakfast this very morning?

"But is that what they mean?" She hesitated and his frown deepened. What else could it mean? "We're not sharing a bed," she clarified.

"And we won't be." Even though their interlude in the

kitchen had left him half erect for the rest of dinner, which had made it damn difficult to carry on a conversation with her brothers.

And then after, in his room... When she'd slammed the door behind her, he'd been simmering from their kiss and their fight. So he'd slipped the tongue of his belt loose, let the heavy buckle hang free. A flick and a jerk had his fly open, and he'd pulled his cock through the opening in his boxers, not even taking the time to pull any of his clothes down. He wrapped his fist around his hard-on as tightly as she would have. Or maybe not even as tightly—she was all fire and fury when she came at him, nothing tentative or hesitant in her touch. He'd loved that she was the one woman who met his physicality measure for measure.

If she hadn't stopped them, he might have pinned her against the wall with enough force to rattle both their teeth. He'd have given her no time to catch her breath, would have been inside her in half a heartbeat. And she'd have raked her nails down his back hard enough to hurt, to let him know how much she liked it.

He'd imagined all that as he fisted his cock, alone in his room, eyes shut tight as he worked himself toward a quick, juddering climax. An unsatisfying climax since she wasn't sharing it with him.

"Ms. Merrill?"

The nurse's brisk summons jerked him out of his imaginings.

She led them back to an examination room, cold and sterile as these places usually were. A chart on the wall showed a baby at various stages of development, from a fish-like thing, to alien terror, then finally something almost human. Adriano sat with his back to it as Lil settled herself on the exam table, the paper crinkling loudly as she did.

"Take off your clothes," the nurse ordered, "and put on the gown." She shut the door behind her as she left.

Lil stared at him. He stared back.

"Do you... do you want me to turn around?" he asked. It seemed ridiculous—they *had* made a baby together—but suddenly they felt like nothing more than strangers here in this room.

"Don't be silly." But she didn't sound as if she found it amusing, her shoulders hunched as if trying to hide from him.

"I'd prefer to." And truly he would. Seeing that body that he hungered for but couldn't touch...

Do not get a hard-on at the doctor's office.

"Oh. Well, if it makes you feel better." She raised her hands to her shirt buttons and he turned his head just in time to miss seeing any skin. Her clothing rustled as she removed it, his gaze hard on the cold white enamel of the sink as his ears caught every whisper of cloth moving across her skin.

He'd undressed her slowly that last night in Vegas. Their couplings had been rushed and wild and frantic. But that last time, with the sadness of farewell between them— everything had slowed.

And now he was averting his gaze from the sight of her that he craved.

"You can look." Her voice was solemn without a hint of teasing.

The shapeless hospital gown was falling off one of her shoulders, and an absurd paper sheet was covering her thighs, leaving the curves of her knees and calves bare. No doubt she was entirely naked beneath that thin paper covering.

His forehead broke out in a sweat.

"See? All decent." Ah, there was the teasing now, a green spark of amusement dancing in her gray gaze.

He smiled, but didn't laugh.

I would have laughed at this in Brazil. I laughed more there.

The thought brought him up short. He had, hadn't he? When he'd first come here, he remembered laughing at almost everything. But as his winnings grew bigger, his training more intense, his focus even tighter—the laughter had slipped away somewhere. But that was not something to ponder here.

A rap at the door and then the doctor came in.

She was a middle-aged woman with a graying bob, crisp in her white coat with a stethoscope draped round her neck. She shook Lil's hand first. "I'm Dr. Young. So pleased to meet you, Liliana." The doctor's movements were those of a woman who was confident in herself and her knowledge. "And you must be the dad."

Dad. That was a new one to hang on to him. "I am. I'm Adriano."

Dr. Young shook his hand, then settled onto a stool by the computer and began flipping through the novel Liliana had filled out. "Good, good," she muttered to herself. "Was this pregnancy planned?"

When she looked up, her gaze was free of judgment. No doubt she asked this of every couple who came before her.

Adriano still felt his face heat. Lil was staring at her hands. "No," they said together, Lil sounding as shamed as he did.

"Hmm." The doctor frowned down at the chart. "You left the bit about living together blank. *Are* you two living together?"

"Yes," Adriano said firmly at the same time Lil said, "Kind of. We're trying it out."

They'd have to practice their lies together if they didn't want to let it slip about their unusual bargain.

Dr. Young's gaze bounced from Lil to him and back again. "Well, good luck to you."

"Thanks," Adriano said. They'd need it.

The doctor looked as if she might be trying not to smile. She set aside the novel and said, "Time for the physical exam."

What followed was the most excruciating fifteen minutes of Adriano's life. He'd never had a routine exam at the doctor—setting broken bones didn't count as routine care—and he'd never imagined the invasive hell a woman went through. Fingers poking, pinching, and prodding everywhere, a thing called a speculum that had come straight from the Inquisition, and as a final insult, something the doctor called a cervical smear.

Adriano looked to the floor for that and breathed heavily, all the questions he'd meant to ask wiped away. Thank God he hadn't eaten anything since breakfast. Forget having bones set—being a woman at a routine visit was a thousand times worse.

Lil didn't make a peep, as if all this was normal and right. Good thing she was the one having the baby, because Adriano never could have stood something like this.

He hoped the baby's care would be less invasive than this. It had to be, didn't it?

"All right," the doctor said with a satisfied snap of her gloves. "Time for the ultrasound."

Lil began to push herself up, clutching at the shoulder of her gown to keep it on. In half a second he was by her side, one hand at her back to help her up. His fingers settled on the warm, bare skin exposed by the opening in the gown. He ignored the urge to trail them along her spine and instead busied himself with arranging the gown more securely around her.

"Are you all right?" he asked as quietly as he could. It wasn't entirely for show, although she might think so—he really was concerned after all she'd just been through.

"Yeah. Don't worry, the worst part is over," she said, as quiet as he. She primly smoothed the paper sheet draped over her legs. "Thank you."

He sat back down as the doctor wheeled over the ultrasound machine.

"We're already going to see the baby?" Lil asked. He could hear her trying for excitement, but unease pulled her shoulders in toward each other.

"Yep." Dr. Young gestured to Adriano. "Come up and sit by Liliana's head so you can see."

Adriano went where he was told. Whatever was about to happen, it couldn't be as bad as that exam. Lil had said that the worst was over.

The doctor flipped up Lil's gown, leaving her belly exposed while the paper sheet covered everything below her hips.

Adriano felt doubly exposed at the sight of Lil's bare skin, being here with her yet not *with* her, and the paper seemed to shield him from unease as much as it did her.

The questions he'd been holding in came rushing to his tongue. "Should her belly be so small? Is it bad that it took so long to find out she was pregnant? What should she be eating? What kind of exercises can she do? What shouldn't she be doing?"

Dr. Young blinked at him as her mouth fell open. Lil wrapped her fingers around her wrist and dug her fingernails in. *Watch it.*

He ignored the sting. It was his child too; he had a right to ask questions of the doctor.

"Well," the doctor began, "I'm not worried about the size of her belly. Lil is pretty slim and this is her first, so it might be a while before she shows." Dr. Young gave Lil a quick smile. "While we usually see patients starting at eight weeks, seeing someone at twelve weeks—like Lil is—isn't so bad. As for the rest of it, we'll get to that. Don't you want to see the baby first?"

He tugged his wrist out of Lil's grip. "Yes."

Lil flashed him one last glare, then turned her attention back to Dr. Young.

The doctor rubbed the wand over her stomach, pressing deeply, white fuzz flashing on the ultrasound screen. The pressure Dr. Young was applying must have been uncomfortable, but Liliana didn't flinch, only kept her gaze hard on the screen. The doctor seemed to know what she was seeing, but to Adriano, it looked no more like the insides of a body than a TV test pattern did.

Dr. Young shoved the wand this way and that into Lil's belly, stopping every so often to take a picture of the fuzz or measure something. Disappointment rose in Adriano. In the movies, parents always saw a perfect picture of their baby, their expressions instantly filling with love and devotion. But he saw nothing here that looked anything like anything. Nothing that might inspire such feelings in him.

Then he caught a glimpse of something that looked like fingers.

"Was that—?" It couldn't be. The baby was only a few months along. How could it already have fingers?

"Yep." The doctor moved the wand, and five fingers and a hand appeared. "That's an arm."

Suddenly the enormity of it hit Adriano. There was a

person inside Lil, a person he'd helped make. A person he'd be responsible for for the rest of his life. And he'd learned about it only two days ago.

Not quite the moment in the movies—he wasn't filled with unending wonder—but a profound realization all the same.

"Is the baby all right?" he asked. There should be more than simply an arm in there.

"As far as I can tell," the doctor said. "But if something is wrong at this stage, there's not much we can do." She didn't look away from the ultrasound screen.

Lil sucked in a breath, and Adriano found himself reaching for her hand, gripping tightly. He'd only just discovered this baby, but hearing that there might be nothing to be done...

He wanted this child. Wanted it more fiercely than he'd ever wanted anything else.

Dr. Young kept on prodding Lil with the wand, going past what looked like legs, up the torso, and stopped at a head that looked entirely human. No fish or alien here. "Do you want to know the sex?"

Lil turned to stare at him. He stared back, unable to decipher her expression. Her eyes were wide—perhaps a yes—but her mouth curved down—perhaps a no.

"Whichever you prefer," he said. Girl, boy—it didn't matter to him. What mattered was that the child was his.

"Okay," Lil said, uncertainty stretching the word.

"Well, she looks fine so far," the doctor announced.

She? "You can already tell that?" Adriano asked.

"Yep," Dr. Young said, years of assurance behind that one word. "There's a slight chance I'm wrong"—clearly she thought it very slight—"but you're having a little girl."

He would have a daughter. Adriano wasn't certain how he

felt about that—the immense pressure in his chest couldn't be named as any kind of emotion he'd felt before—so he concentrated on how his mother would feel. She'd be delighted by the promise of a new granddaughter.

Yes, best to focus on his mother's delight and not the overpowering sensation trying to crush him.

A little girl.

Lil was staring at the screen, looking as stunned as he felt. No joy, no excitement—only a numbed shock. He couldn't fault her for that, not when he felt the same way.

The doctor set the wand aside and wiped Lil's belly. "We'll be more certain at the anatomy ultrasound in several weeks. Any other questions until your next appointment in four weeks?"

"She won't have an appointment for four weeks?" That didn't sound right at all. "Shouldn't you be seeing her at least once a week?" Where was this impressive medical care Americans bragged about? Lil was wealthy and she should be getting the best.

Dr. Young laughed—actually laughed. "No. She'll be fine. I should say, since you're trying to live together, that sexual relations are fine. I recommend you use a barrier method of protection until your STD test results come back. But the nurse will draw blood from the both of you before you leave."

Adriano went rigid, felt Lil stiffen next to him. He swallowed hard, flexed his fist, and glanced at her. Her expression was unreadable, which was unusual for her.

"Is there anything else that's allowed?" she asked dryly.

He recognized her aim—she was referring to the book and what it said she couldn't do. Well, the doctor would soon set her straight on the correctness of the book.

"Oh, most everything's allowed," Dr. Young said.

Adriano frowned. *Everything?* The book had made it sound as if nothing was quite safe enough.

"No heavy lifting," the doctor went on, "try not to strain your back. No steam rooms or saunas or hot tubs. Food that's been heated to a safe temperature, no unpasteurized cheese or milk."

There. There was what he'd been looking for.

He tried to keep the triumph from his expression as Lil nodded along.

"Oh," Dr. Young said, waggling a finger, "and no horse-back riding."

Lil blinked as if blinded, then burst into tears.

And Adriano found out that being right wasn't quite as sweet as he'd thought it would be.

LIL WIPED down the kitchen counter one last time, although it had been clean several swipes ago. She was stalling, she knew she was stalling—but she went over the counter one more time.

It had been just her and Adriano at dinner. Luke was off who knew where—probably wining and dining some woman—and Benedict was with Pilar.

And Lil was wasting time in the kitchen so that she wouldn't have to spend the evening alone with the father of her child. Luke and Benedict certainly had better evening plans than she did.

Adriano came into the kitchen with a towel in hand, his expression neutral. "I wiped down the table."

"Thanks." Now what? It was too soon to go to bed. This was the problem with living with a man—you had to figure out what to do with him most of the time. "Do you want to watch TV?"

TV. Always the answer to any question.

"Sure." He sounded about as enthusiastic at the idea as she was.

She took the rag from him and tossed both his and hers into the wash, then followed him into the living room for their evening of unmarried, sexless bliss.

He sat at one end of the long sectional, close enough for her to sense him but not close enough for her to accidentally touch him. Or intentionally either.

She got it. She remembered his rejection of last night.

But the doctor had said sex was perfectly fine...

Stop it. No matter what the doctor had said, sex was right out. There were a thousand reasons why they shouldn't. The chilly atmosphere between them being one. Their bargain being another.

She grabbed the remote. "Is there a show you'd like to watch?" She called up the guide and began to flip through six hundred channels. Nothing caught her interest.

"I don't watch much TV."

No, he probably watched videos of bull rides all day long, studying them to improve his own rides. Lecturing her on her pregnancy and riding bulls seemed to be his only pastimes.

She found a show on natural horsemanship on RFD-TV and left it there. Rather bitter to watch a show about horses when she couldn't ride for the next however many months. But she left it on anyway.

When the doctor had said she couldn't ride, that coupled with seeing the baby had made everything overflow. Her tears had embarrassed Adriano—and her—but she couldn't help it. The dam had burst.

Once she'd quit sniveling, they'd hightailed it out of the doctor's office to drive back to the ranch in silence. She'd run off to her office as soon as she could to do boring, safe paperwork, and he'd... Well, she didn't know what he'd done. She'd been too caught up in her own reaction to think about his.

She could do her job without being on a horse, but handling the bulls was now completely out of the question. Her teeth came hard together, and she only just kept from grinding them. It was her project, and she wasn't going to be shunted off to piddling managerial crap. Except that she totally was, at least until this pregnancy was over.

She slid her back teeth across each other, a tiny scrape, just to sand away some of the frustration.

"We're having a little girl," Adriano said out of nowhere in a stunned tone, as if the fact of it had landed too heavily on his head.

"Yep," she said. There wasn't much else she could think to add. "I guess we'll have to talk about girl names." Names, baby gear—she knew babies needed a lot of stuff, but exactly what stuff?

Her head began to throb, that same hammer of realization that had hit him pounding within her temples.

"Do you have any you like?" he asked, turning to study her.

She didn't. Picking out baby names had never been a hobby of hers. She stared at the TV to avoid the golden knife of his gaze. "No. Do you?"

"My mother's name is very nice."

Her back tensed. They couldn't name the baby after his mom and not have her mom's name too. That was a recipe for fighting. It wasn't *fair*. "So is my mother's." She kept her voice carefully flat, kept her eyes on the TV. The trainer was going on in his Australian drawl about getting the horse to respect him.

Adriano didn't train horses; he rode bulls. And only for a few seconds at a time. There was a metaphor for their relationship in there somewhere.

"I suppose we have some time." His words were as studiedly neutral as hers had been.

"Months and months," she agreed. Months and months to decide on a name, who the baby would go with when. Months and months apart from her daughter while Adriano was with her in Brazil.

She could make those months shorter if she kept to her plan and convinced him she was right—that the baby belonged with her.

Silence stretched between them as the TV droned on. Was this what married couples did? Watched TV and waited for the years to pass? And tried not to argue?

He began to drum his fingers against his thigh, a soft *thrum-thrum-thrum* that made her think too much about the skin and muscle under all that denim. He released a sharp exhale and turned to her again. "I have to fly out again tomorrow."

"What? Already?" She let her jaw hang. How could she prove this life was the best for their child if he wasn't even here to see it?

He sliced a look at her. "There's an event in Nevada. And after that, Colorado. I told you I'd need to keep competing. I can't sit here and wait on you."

Wait on her? Her lip curled. "I never asked you to wait on me. And you might have told me you were leaving before now. When will you be back?"

"I don't know."

Oh, that was it. His too casual tone was a spur to her

anger. "Well, thanks for telling me." The sarcasm in her voice was acidic enough to etch glass.

That pissed him off, his eyes darkening to a furious bronze. But when he spoke, his tone was even. "Remember, you have to eat well. And rest. And don't do anything dangerous."

Somehow the fact that he was putting on this caring-dad act to help win their bargain made her fury flare. "How could I forget? That's all you ever harp on me about." The cooking, eating breakfast, training the bulls—him being right about some of it made her want to punch something. "Don't try to tie me down. I'll buck harder than any bull you've ever ridden."

"Huh." A short noise of disbelief, a spark of intrigue lighting his eyes. "As if any man could tie you down."

"No. No man could." Being tied, being restrained, held no allure for her. She wanted a man who met her as an equal in everything.

For one wild weekend in Vegas, that man had been Adriano.

"A man might want to try." He canted toward her, his focus sharpening on her.

"He could try," she taunted. "But he'd never succeed."

That was all it took. He was over her, pushing her back into the couch, his mouth on hers. No hesitation, no fumbling, just the way she liked it. A man who wanted as much as she did.

His lips were soft, but the intent behind them was hard.

She parted her lips, sent her tongue into his mouth, her need meeting his measure for measure. He gave a ragged sigh and his hand slipped around the back of her neck, gripped tightly. She pulled him back with her onto the couch, spreading her legs to make space for him between them.

His hips were heavy and hot settling into her pelvis, his cock gratifyingly hard. She rubbed against him, her legs sliding up to clasp his thighs, her clit throbbing at the contact.

He wanted her. Badly. Her smile was sharply triumphant. So much for his vow to keep his hands off her.

If she could make him break his vow on this, she could break him on the rest of it. If she simply kept her wits here...

She slid her hands down his back, gripped his ass, and pulled him hard against her, urging him on. *I want you too. Take me. Let me take you.* Wanting wasn't losing her head. Holding him like this meant she was in control. Right?

His mouth dragged down her neck, and he raked his teeth along the sensitive skin there. She dug her fingers into his ass, the taut muscles flexing beneath her grip.

God, they still had their clothes on, and she was already on fire. Too long without him—she'd been too long without him. *Focus.* But the thought was lost in the hot pulses shaking her.

"Liliana, Liliana," he murmured into her neck, his teeth scraping again as his mouth formed the *n* of her name. Sharp teeth, sweet song of her name, his hand still firm on her neck—she was lost, utterly lost, just like she'd been before.

His hand slipped between them, found the skin of her stomach where her shirt had ridden up. She whimpered helplessly as he stroked there, so close yet so far from where she wanted him to be.

"Adriano," she ground out. "You have to touch me. You have to."

Another rough kiss on her neck, a promise that he was

getting there. She lifted her hips, demanded that it be now and hard.

His hand slipped lower, skimmed past her navel, teased above the waist of her jeans, made her throb all the way to her toes. A tug at her waistband let her know that finally, finally he was getting to where he was supposed to be. She rubbed against him in encouragement, and moaned deep when his hard cock caught her clit just right. The second his fingers touched her she was going to come, she just knew it. The waves were already rising, her thighs trembling beneath his.

The waistband of her jeans cut into her back as he fumbled with the buttons, a sharp, rough pressure in contrast to the heavy, luxuriant weight of his hips at her front.

"What the—?" He lifted his head and frowned at her, holding up the hair tie that had held her jeans closed.

"Oh. My jeans... they wouldn't close this morning." Although her stomach looked about the same, when she'd gone to zip up her jeans, the two sides wouldn't meet. A reminder that while things might look the same, they most certainly weren't beneath the surface.

She scrambled up, put distance between him and her, then cupped her forehead. *Idiot.* She just had to make things difficult for herself, didn't she?

Her control of the situation had been an illusion from the first moment his lips had touched hers.

His gaze was tight on her, his lungs working hard, his jaw grim. The bulge in his Wranglers told her he was as physically aroused as she.

But just because he had a hard-on, it didn't mean he didn't have darker motives here. He meant to convince her to give up her baby.

She'd forgotten that in the molten rush between them. She couldn't forget herself with him—they had a bargain. One she had to win.

"We're not supposed to be doing this." Stark. But not as cold as she might have liked. She took a shaky breath, summoned her temper, her restraint—anything to cool the fire still licking at her veins.

"I didn't hear you saying no." Colder than she'd managed.

Fucker. "Really? I didn't hear you saying it either." *Damn me for this and you damn yourself as well.*

He blinked, his mouth turning down. She'd hit with that one. "You make me want you too much."

Nope. Try again. She rose from the couch. "Please. Don't pull that tired crap with me. You're a grown man. I know you know how to say no." She drew the *no* out to prove exactly how easy it was to say.

"Fine." He rose, his cock straining against his fly. "No."

"I said it first."

He actually laughed. A short one that he immediately smothered—but definitely a laugh. "Now that we've worked out that we can both say no, I'll wish you good night. I have an early flight."

There was a question for him in her throat, but it wouldn't take shape. Probably because she wasn't entirely sure what to ask: *Will you call? When will you be back? Promise me you'll be safe?* All foolish, relationship-type questions. They didn't have a relationship—they had a bargain.

"Good night," was all she said, forcing it past that unformed question stuck in her throat.

Nothing more was said as they made their way to their separate beds.

Chapter 7

TO: Liliana Merrill

From: Adriano Silva

How are you feeling? Did you eat breakfast? How much coffee did you drink? How did you sleep? You should be recording all this for your doctor's visit. Remember, it's all to keep the baby as safe as we can.

TO: Adriano Silva

From: Liliana Merrill

I'm great, thanks for asking! How was your flight on this trip you told me about at the very last minute?

TO: Liliana Merrill

From: Adriano Silva

There's no need for sarcasm. What did you eat today? How much water did you drink? It's very important that you drink enough water.

(And it doesn't matter how my flight was—your health is

more important. But it was fine, thank you. I arrived in Reno safely.)

TO: Adriano Silva

From: Liliana Merrill

I'm attaching the spreadsheet with all my meals and water intake for your approval. I've also begun to keep track of the frequency and color of my urine since I'm sure you'll ask about that next.

TO: Liliana Merrill

From: Adriano Silva

The spreadsheet was empty. Perhaps you attached the wrong one? And the book doesn't say anything about tracking your urine. Do you really think you should?

TO: Adriano Silva

From: Liliana Merrill

Look, I'm eating just fine. I've got protein, fruit, veggies, and some starch at every meal. And only one cup of coffee every day, although the headaches have been a bitch. Maybe you can trust me to feed myself? I've been doing it for a while now.

(Did you get to Colorado safely?)

TO: Liliana Merrill

From: Adriano Silva

You're feeding the baby now as well—don't forget that. What kind of prenatal vitamin are you taking? Does it have the DHEA? The book says that's very important for the baby's brain.

(Yes, got to Denver just fine. First go round is tonight.)

TO: Adriano Silva

From: Liliana Merrill

I got whatever generic kind the drugstore had. And yes, it's got the extra DHEA, although that pill makes me gag every time. See how I sacrifice for the baby already?

(I heard you got hurt. Is everything okay?)

TO: Liliana Merrill

From: Adriano Silva

I just read on BabyBumper.com that green tea might be bad for the baby. Please make certain you're not drinking it.

(I only sprained my elbow. I can still ride, although it hurts like a son of a bitch. But don't worry, I'm fine.)

TO: Adriano Silva

From: Liliana Merrill

Okay, this has gone way too far. You need to stop reading that website. And the book too. You think everything and anything could harm the baby. If it were up to you, I'd be in an isolation ward "for the baby's health."

Just stop.

(And I'm glad you're okay.)

TO: Liliana Merrill

From: Adriano Silva

There's no need for hysterics.

TO: Adriano Silva
From: Liliana Merrill
You did NOT just call me hysterical.

TO: Liliana Merrill
From: Adriano Silva
You must stay calm for the baby. She feels your stress, and too much cortisol could damage her brain.

TO: Adriano Silva
From: Liliana Merrill
(Never Sent)
I will show you *stress* and *hysteria* when I see you next. I will shove *stress* and *hysteria* so far up your butt you choke on them. Of all the pigheaded, messed-up things to say to a pregnant woman...

TO: Liliana Merrill
From: Adriano Silva
You haven't sent me a food log this week. And you should also keep track of when you feel nauseated or when you throw up. More nausea is better for the baby.

TO: Adriano Silva
From: Liliana Merrill
No.

. . .

TO: Liliana Merrill
From: Adriano Silva

I think your previous message was cut off. Look, if you haven't been keeping track of your food, you can just start now. We'll forget about all the other days you haven't kept a record and start fresh.

TO: Liliana Merrill
From: Adriano Silva
Liliana? Did you get my message?

TO: Liliana Merrill
From: Adriano Silva
Liliana?

TO: Liliana Merrill
From: Adriano Silva
Lil?

ADRIANO CHECKED his e-mail on his phone for the fifth time that morning. Still nothing from Liliana.

He wandered through the bleachers under the covered arena, watched as the cowboys set up for that night's event. He had nothing better to do than to wait. Wait for the event tonight and wait for Lil to finally respond to him.

Actually, there was something he could do. He sat on

one of the benches, the metal cold in the morning air, and brought up his mother's number, the ringing scratchy as it sounded across the miles.

"Adriano!"

He smiled. "How did you know it was me?"

"The phone says it's you, silly boy." The familiarity of her voice made his heart ache. "I love that about these mobile phones. I know who's calling before I even pick up. I know to be excited for you, to be resigned for Dara since she talks so much, and stern with Roberto since he'll be asking for money."

Adriano laughed. He was glad to hear her so happy about the phone he'd gotten her, safe and comfortable in the house he'd bought her. She wasn't too fond of its location in Campo Grande—the city was too large, too loud for her liking—but once he returned, he'd move her to the ranch he would buy. That would please her.

"I'm glad to talk to you too." He rubbed at his thigh, bending his head to hold in the sound of her a little better. "How are you, *Mamãe*?"

"Better, now that I've spoken to you. I was feeling tired, but that's all gone, to hear you laugh. You hardly laugh at all now. I miss it."

"I laugh." But he knew she was right. "Have you been taking your medicine?"

"How could I forget when you're always reminding me?" But she liked it, her adult children fussing over her.

If only he could be there to properly care for her. But the money he sent made it possible for the medical care. And someday the transplant would come through. He had to believe that. That he wouldn't lose her before he could return home.

"Tell me, how is Liliana?" she asked.

"Good." At least he thought she was. He e-mailed her several times a day, asking how she was, showing how caring, how concerned he could be—and it wasn't an act. But over the weeks, her answers had grown shorter and shorter, as if his concern irritated her. And then the e-mail he'd sent last night, still unanswered...

He could call her, but he wanted to hear her voice, wanted it very badly, so he hadn't, telling himself it would only be distracting. After their last encounter, he'd realized she remained too tempting—close contact with her obliterated his focus.

But if she didn't reply soon, he'd have to call to make certain she was all right.

He didn't want to discuss any of this with his mother. "Did you get the picture of the baby I sent?"

"I'm looking at it right now. She'll be so beautiful, my son. I can already tell." Love swelled in his mother's voice.

Adriano slipped his hand into his shirt pocket and fished out the sonogram picture, the same one he'd sent to his mother, the same one he stared at every night before he fell asleep.

"She'll be the prettiest girl this world has ever seen." He knew it was true without even having seen his daughter. Her skin would be lighter than his but darker than her mother's, her mouth a soft pink bow, her hair dark and curling, and her eyes... There was no telling what color her eyes would be. One of his grandfathers had had green eyes, much like Liliana's. There was no way to know until their daughter was here.

Only five more months. An eternity. And too short. He had a long way to go to win this bargain with Lil, judging by the responses to his messages.

Only one more day here in Colorado and then he could

fly back to California. Three weeks until the next event; Oklahoma next time. He could patch things up with Lil, explain that the e-mails were for her own good, then move on to the next event, move forward with his plan to finish in the top ten this year.

"She has the world's most handsome father," his mother was saying, "so of course she will be."

Adriano laughed again. "I bet you told Rodrigo and João that too."

"Well, they're my sons as well. The three most handsome boys in the world and all three my sons." She was laughing now herself.

"We can't all be the most handsome," he said. "There can be only one. You'll have to pick."

She sighed gustily. "Well, if I must... It's you. But don't tell your brothers I said that."

"Of course not. Because you'll tell them the same when you talk to them next."

The sound of his mother's laughter warmed him from the inside out. His loneliness here, the long, stony days of training, training, training, and nothing but—it was all worth it to hear his mother so happy. And it would be even more worth it when his daughter came and he could provide her with the childhood he never had. Could show her the beauty of Mato Grosso do Sul and raise her with her loving grandmother, aunts, uncles, and cousins surrounding her.

"I miss you," his mother said, her words holding the lingering glow of her laughter but also tinged with wistfulness.

"I miss you too. But you'll come when the baby's born, won't you?"

A terrible promise to extract from his mother, to force

her to fly so far when she was ill. But if Lil had full custody…
His mother had to be there if she could.

"Of course I'll come," his mother said. "I'll want to hold this new granddaughter of mine."

God, he wished he could be as certain as she was.

There was a commotion on her end of the line, followed by high, childish voices shouting hello.

"Ah, Elena and the children are here." Elena was his other sister, bringing her children to visit their *vovó*. He could hear his mother's attention turn from him. If he were there with her, he could greet his nieces and nephews as well, spend some time with them. Instead, he'd have to hang up and spend the rest of his day waiting for the bull ride at the end.

The loneliness was worth it, but it still hurt.

"Tell them I said hello." He forced himself to sound happy. "And I'll talk to you tomorrow."

"They say hello themselves. I love you, son. Take care of yourself around those dangerous animals you ride."

He laughed. "Those dangerous animals make me a lot of money." Before she could comment on that, he said, "I love you too. Good-bye."

Adriano stayed on the bench a moment longer, watching the cowboys assemble the chutes. They groaned as they set the fence panels into place, the metal tubes clanging as they met. A bull sent up a bellow from somewhere outside the covered arena.

The air was filled with the scent of dust and cattle and manure and heat, the same as the arenas had smelled at home. No matter where he went, cattle—and bulls—were all much the same. Only this event was going to have more money at the end of it than any at home had had.

If he kept a clear head, kept his focus on the bull, he'd

win some of that money. He needed to—the past two events he'd barely finished in the money. His focus had been hazy, his mind only half on his riding. The other half had been with Lil and their daughter.

He checked his e-mail again. Nothing.

He could call her—he wanted to call her. Wanted the bright brashness of her voice to fill the loneliness in him.

A dangerous urge, that. He ought to be thinking of how to win their bargain, how to prove that the baby was better off with him. Not wallowing in this useless longing for her.

Useless or not, it wasn't leaving. It had been a constant companion these weeks away from her.

Slowly, he rose, waving to the workers in the arena as he walked past. He went outside to where the trailers were parked, found where Miguel was holding court under a pop-up tent, about a dozen Brazilians forming a circle around him.

"Adriano," he called. "How are you?"

"Well enough." Adriano took an empty seat and the soda someone handed him. He couldn't complain—all of these men were in the same boat he was, a boat far from home.

"Are you coming back to the ranch after this?" Miguel asked.

Between events, Adriano had gone back to Miguel's ranch these past two weeks. Easier to do that than haul all the way back to California. And he could train with his friends there.

Lil had still been answering his messages at that point, letting him know everything was all right.

Adriano checked his phone. Still nothing.

He sighed. "No, I need to go see Lil." Everything was probably fine and she was simply pissed at him about something, but he had to find out. Even if he feared the wildfire of his response to her. Even if his riding suffered further because of it.

Miguel nodded. "How's the baby?"

"Fine." *I think.*

"These first pregnancies are always the worst," Miguel said.

Many of the other men nodded. Adriano had told them about the baby and word had slowly been filtering through the rest of the bull riders. Most everyone had congratulated him, although there had been more than few raised eyebrows when he'd said who the mother was.

Crane, that asshole, had laughed in his grating way and said something about happy accidents and how Adriano had hit pay dirt. Adriano had pretended not to understand him. Again.

His phone buzzed in his pocket. He fished it out, checked his e-mail. *Liliana.* Finally.

He opened the message and read it. Just two words there. He frowned and read it again.

The meaning wasn't entirely clear, but the intent behind those two words were: Lil was pissed. Extremely pissed.

Wonderful. That was going to be just wonderful for his concentration tonight. But at least she was okay.

He might not be though, once he finally made it back to her side.

THE E-MAIL NOTIFICATION on Lil's phone buzzed. Again.

She fished the phone out of her pocket and flicked it to mute, shoved it back and sat down hard on it. Stupid phone. It could be quiet for a while. She already knew exactly who was e-mailing her and what it would say. After her two-word reply to Adriano this morning, he was probably very, very pissed. But she was sick of him carping on her through e-mail.

Multiple times a day he sent those messages—nothing soft or sweet. Or even slightly human. Just demands that she eat properly, sleep enough, was she throwing up enough—morning sickness was a good thing, apparently—and similar dictates along those lines.

Never a call, never any indication that she was anything more than a baby incubator to him. It got depressing after a while. Which made her mad.

Putting her chin in her hands, she slumped in the folding chair, or tried to slump. Her belly made it hard since it seemed there was less and less room for her organs as the baby grew. She could only smush things together so far anymore.

She was watching Beau and Diego train a bull to enter the chute. Beau had ridden bulls too until a shoulder injury sent him into early retirement and back into Penny's arms—Penny being one of the Moreno cousins and the ranch vet. Thank goodness he had, since Lil was able to hire Beau on to help with the bucking-bull operation.

And thank goodness Beau could take over these training tasks she couldn't do anymore. This training ensured a bull was quiet and well mannered during transport, behind the chutes, and on the way to them.

And once that gate swung open, the bull had to become a demon.

Not that any of the training was going to be worth a damn if she couldn't get this bull on the circuit. She'd very politely asked the committee if they'd reconsider the two bulls she'd offered them last week but hadn't heard back yet. She'd even made certain the e-mail went to James White's personal address, an old friend of her dad's and a member of the committee. It stung her pride to make that personal appeal to him, but it wasn't like pride hadn't gotten her anywhere so far.

Look at her now, sitting on the sidelines instead of helping train her bull. She was about as useless as tits on a boar here. But it was better than sitting in the office, crunching numbers. The average person might think there wasn't a lot of accounting to be done in a stock operation, but they'd be dead wrong.

"I'm heading out," she called to Beau. "Is this it for today?"

"Yep. One last trip into the chute for this boy, then he's done. You got big plans for tonight?"

"Ha. Bea and I are going to get together and watch TV."

Beau smiled. "Sounds pretty tame for you."

It was. Staying in wasn't how Lil used to spend her Friday nights. Raising hell at the Stampede was how she preferred to do things. But considering the size of her belly —which had strangely swelled to the size of a basketball over the past two weeks—and the fact she couldn't drink, going to a bar was out. Instead, she was playing sad single mom at home, accompanied by her spinster cousin. Woe was her.

"See you Monday," she called to them both. "Have a good weekend."

Once she was at the house, she ate a frozen dinner—but one packed with veggies—choked down a prenatal vitamin, and ignored the e-mail pop-ups on her phone with a force that impressed even herself.

When Bea finally arrived, Lil was ready to climb the walls. "What do you want to do?" she demanded the instant Bea walked through the door.

"What can you do?" Bea tossed down her purse, took one of the mugs of tea Lil had made.

"God, you sound like Adriano. I'm not an invalid, you know." She wasn't certain if she was directing that solely at Bea or at one pigheaded bull rider who was hundreds of miles away.

"Things are going that well?" Bea took a smug sip from her mug.

"Things are going terribly. You should see the messages he sends me. He's trying to rule my life remotely."

"Rule your life?" Bea raised an eyebrow, that disloyal thing. "Maybe you're being a bit melodramatic?"

"No. Look at this." Lil called up a particularly irritating one from yesterday.

"'What are you eating?'" she read off, doing her best imitation of whiny Adriano. "'You have to keep track so you know if you're taking in enough iron. Are you avoiding soy? Make sure you don't drink more than one cup of coffee. What's your weight today? How much sleep did you get last night?'" She raised her eyebrows. "Do you see?"

"Maybe he's just trying to show his concern." But her cousin's mouth was pinched up with distaste. Good old Bea, always playing devil's advocate.

"How would you appreciate something like this?" Lil countered. She was guessing Bea would be just as pissed as she was.

"Okay, so it is pretty off-putting," Bea admitted. *Point: Lil.* "What did you reply?"

"*Get bent.*" Just two little words, but it covered pretty much everything she wanted Adriano Silva to do with himself and his overbearing e-mails. He'd take it as ammunition in his fight to take the baby, but she didn't care at this point. His controlling nature was all the ammunition she needed in *her* fight to keep the baby with her.

Now it was Bea's turn to raise her eyebrows. "Does that really translate to Portuguese?"

"If he doesn't understand what it means, I'll show him when he gets back." Whenever that might be. There'd been no mention of his return in any of his sucky messages. Not that she'd been obsessing over it, a tingle running through her when she thought of seeing him again. Not at all. That was relationship-type stuff.

"When is he coming back?"

"I don't know. He hasn't said." Which didn't bode well for any future co-parenting. Was he going to disappear into Brazil with her daughter and never say when she was coming back?

Somehow Lil didn't really think so, but sometimes, when she was really pissed at him—usually after getting one of his e-mails—she liked to pretend she believed it. The pretense made her anger seem more justified.

Of course, Lil could pick up the phone, call one of the lawyers the family had on retainer. Simply pass the entire situation off to a legal team.

But she hadn't. Because she just had to make things harder for herself.

"Huh." Bea tilted her head, assumed her "concerned scientist" look. "Was he like this in Vegas? You usually don't go for the emotionally unavailable control freak type."

"No, he... he laughed then." Not a ton, but she distinctly remembered him laughing. "And he *talked* to me—not just demanded a food log."

He'd treated her like a person then, a person he was fiercely attracted to, and not an incubator he was trying to tweak to bake the most perfect baby.

"Huh." Bea chewed on that. "Huh."

Not a great contribution. "Did you know they call him Slick Eddie on the circuit?"

"Who told you that?"

"Beau." Lil had wormed that out of Beau one day while they were watching one of Adriano's rides on YouTube. To see the bull he'd been riding, not him of course.

Bea wrinkled her nose. "Eddie? That's not even his name."

"I guess it's the closest nickname to Adriano. I agree, it's ridiculous," Lil said at Bea's look. "But when I asked Beau why they called him slick, he said it was because Adriano wasn't slick at all. That he planned out every aspect of his rides, trained harder than anyone else, studied more videos —Beau said he was a machine."

A machine who wanted to take her baby back to Brazil to raise on his own. *Good luck with that, Silva.*

"Maybe they should have nicknamed him Terminator instead," Bea said.

"Too confusing. That's already the name of a bull."

Her cousin shook her head. "Okay, fine, so you've been impregnated by the Terminator. What now?"

The ten-million-dollar question. "I don't know," Lil confessed. "I did tell him to get bent, but really, I can't just push him out of my life. Or rather, I don't want to." She sighed.

Her brothers would be pretty happy if she did push Adriano out, but somehow she couldn't summon the will to do it. She still had this crazy dream that they might be able to work it all out amicably, that he would agree to her custody arrangement with a smile. That they wouldn't be fighting over this baby for the next eighteen years.

She'd thought having him around all the time, underfoot and demanding her attention, would be bad, but this was worse. He wasn't even here, but he was still managing to infuriate her. That took real talent.

"Lil, I know you suggested that he move in and that you wanted to meet him halfway on the baby... but it sounds like you don't really believe you can."

She hadn't revealed their bargain even to Bea, instead spinning some story about them "working things out."

Adriano had said he would take care of her, but this was the worst possible version of that. If this was what he thought counted as caring and concerned, they were farther apart than he'd ever know.

"I do want to meet him halfway"—not entirely a lie —"but he wants things solely on his terms."

Just as she wanted things solely on hers.

She ought to call the lawyers. Stop making things harder for herself. In fact, that's exactly what she'd do come Monday morning.

"To be fair," Bea said, putting on her devil's advocate hat again, "you've never been a great one for compromise yourself."

Her cousin had a point, but—"I've tried to talk to him, but he puts his spurs to me as if I were a bull he was trying to tame."

Only a hint of an exaggeration there. Purely for effect, of course.

Bea sighed. "I've never met him, so I'll have to take your word for it. I don't want you to be unhappy, but I also don't want you to have to raise this baby all on your own."

"I won't be alone. I have all of my family." And Adriano had his family in Brazil, family as eager to meet this baby as hers was. And his mom, who might not be here too much longer...

Lil clenched her fist. She couldn't let her guilt over that sway her. She had to focus on what was best for the baby.

Bea's expression softened. "Of course we'll all help any way that we can. We love you and we already love the baby."

A lump formed in Lil's throat. Bea really was sweet when she wanted to be.

"But we're not the baby's father," she finished.

Her cousin could also cut right to the quick when she wanted to.

Point: Bea. And Adriano.

"Yeah. I know. Thanks for talking this out with me, but we're not getting anywhere." Lil blew out a resigned breath and fiddled with her phone. "That's enough bitching about my situation. What do you want to watch tonight?"

"I don't know. I don't even really like TV."

"And your favorite band is one I've probably never heard of," Lil muttered.

"What?" Bea frowned in confusion.

"Never mind." Hipsters never admitted they were hipsters. "So we'll just sit here and be surly?" Which they'd kind of already been doing. Although Lil wanted to have fun, to forget for a few hours that her life was such a tangle.

Wallowing was all well and good, but she was ready to move past that. *I'll show you, Silva.*

Which was silly, because he wasn't even here, and he certainly wasn't her boyfriend—but she still wanted to rub her disdain in his face.

"Do you have a better idea?" Bea asked.

Not exactly, but one might be forming. Lil tapped the screen of her phone as she pondered. "Before this pregnancy, I spent my Friday nights having fun."

"Yeah, you also spent them drinking." Bea did not sound like she was up for the kind of fun Lil had in mind.

"You don't have to drink to have fun," Lil said primly.

"Now you sound like some kind of after-school special."

She *had* gotten that line from an after-school special. "I'm serious," she insisted. "We can still dance and whoop it up, even if we're not drinking."

The more Lil thought on it, the better it sounded. Meet some friends, take some turns around the dance floor, share stories—not even Adriano could object to that. The bar part might get him riled, but she wouldn't be drinking. She could even be the designated driver.

"I don't whoop it up," Bea said sourly.

"No, but Penny does. Let's call her. I bet you she'll meet us at the Stampede." In fact, Penny and Beau might already be on their way there. The dance hall held a special place in their hearts.

"Is this really such a good idea with your condition?" All matronly condescension. Cute, considering that Bea had never been pregnant herself.

"My condition? When did you turn into Adriano?"

That one hit. Bea grimaced, but she went for her phone anyway. "Okay, okay, I'll call Penny."

Yes. Dancing and laughing and hanging out would be the best cure for her this evening. She grabbed Bea and pulled her into a two-step in the middle of the kitchen.

"Lil, I'm on the phone!"

Lil only tightened her grip and hummed louder until Bea was laughing too hard to even breathe.

"Hello? Hello?" came from the phone. "Who is this? Bea?"

"Penny!" Lil yelled toward the phone. "We're going to the Stampede! Be ready in twenty minutes."

Bea was still laughing, tripping over her own feet. Lil

spun her one last time, then let her cousin go to catch her own breath.

"See?" She was laughing almost as hard as Bea was. "You do whoop it up."

"I guess I do." Bea straightened. "But only when you force me to."

"I'm going to tonight." Lil grabbed her keys. "Let's go honky-tonking!"

Just saying the words made her feel better than she had in weeks.

Chapter 8

THE RANCH HOUSE WAS DARK and silent when Adriano went through the front door.

It had been a long flight from Colorado, and all he wanted was some supper and to collapse into bed. And to make certain Lil was all right.

He flicked on the entry light and took a tentative step forward. Worry urged him on, but he remembered that last message of hers: *Get bent.* Lil might decide to demonstrate the exact meaning on him.

"Lil?"

Only echoes answered him. Then a faint bark. And another, growing louder, and a scrabbling noise like claws on tile.

Rufio came bounding out of the dark and leaped straight into Adriano's arms. He caught the dog with a grunt, the fuzzy body wriggling with joy as Rufio tried to lick every inch of Adriano's face.

"Hey," he said, "I'm happy to see you too. But don't lick my face off."

Rufio just wriggled harder. After the welcome, or lack of

one, Adriano had been expecting, the dog's happiness was a pleasant surprise. He missed having a dog greet him—no human he knew ever got so excited to see him.

He set Rufio down. "Where's your mistress?"

The dog didn't answer, just stared back at him.

"You're no help. Let's go find her then."

Wandering through the house looking for Lil made him realize just how large the house really was. Room after empty, dark room, with no answer to his calls. Not even her brother was there.

Adriano had known she'd be pissed, but he'd at least hoped she'd have made dinner, something as savory as the gratin and chops she'd made before. She'd gripe at him while he filled his belly with her good cooking, and then he could soothe her ruffled feelings. Not a warm homecoming, exactly, but better than this. This was like coming back to an empty hotel room, his only temporarily, with no one to care if he was here or somewhere else.

Well, there was still Rufio. The dog was happy to see him.

Adriano made his way to the kitchen, the last place to look. She must have left a note somewhere. He'd e-mailed her to tell her he was coming back tonight, so she wouldn't have taken off without leaving a note. Of course, she could have e-mailed or sent a text, which she hadn't.

But there was no note. Nothing to indicate where she'd gone. Fine, she was pissed, but disappearing like this was not acceptable.

He pulled out his phone and called her. One ring. Two rings. And on to five.

"*Hi, this is Lil. Leave a message.*"

He was going to kill her. He shoved his phone back into

his pocket and grabbed his hat. Time to brave the lion's den and see if he could find the mother of his child.

The pool house was as dark and silent as the main house, but Adriano knocked anyway.

There was some scuffling and the sound of something falling—something heavy—and then giggling, probably from a woman. A man grumbled, "Goddamn it, somebody better be dead to interrupt right now."

"Oh, Benedict," the woman chided, still laughing.

Great. Adriano had interrupted their love play. This wasn't at all embarrassing.

When Lil's oldest brother opened his door, he looked about as pissed as Adriano felt.

"If you've come to borrow sugar, we don't have any." Benedict went to slam the door.

Adriano caught the edge of it. "I'm looking for your sister." He pushed against the door, just enough to let Benedict know he was serious.

Benedict pushed back—but he wasn't as strong as Adriano. "She didn't tell you where she was going?"

"No." Would Adriano be here if she had?

"Well," Benedict drawled, "maybe she doesn't want to be found."

Probably true. But Adriano wasn't going to admit that. "She must have forgotten to leave a note."

Benedict the Dick only smiled. "Lil doesn't usually forget things. Maybe you forgot to tell her you were coming back today?"

Do not punch her brother. But God, just a little tap from his fist, just enough to wipe that smirk off Benedict's face. "It seems there was some miscommunication," he said, all smooth confidence. "And it sounds like you don't know where she is either." Now it was his turn to smirk.

That got Benedict riled—he struck Adriano as the kind of man who could never admit he didn't know something. "She's at the Stampede. Her and Bea and Penny."

Jackpot. Now to find this Stampede. He frowned. "That sounds like a bar."

"It is. And a dance hall."

"You let your pregnant sister go to a bar?" What the hell kind of brother did that?

"If you thought I could stop her, then clearly you don't know my sister."

No, Adriano didn't. And that was the entire problem.

He drove to the bar in a controlled, steady fashion. Just because it was a bar didn't mean she was drinking. Just because drunk people did stupid things didn't mean she was in any danger. He repeated that so often he almost, almost believed it.

When he arrived, the parking lot was filled with cars, a knot of smokers out by the front doors. The music was loud even outside, and the stomp of a hundred boot heels pounded in time with a line dance.

Inside, the music banged against his skull, the heat and press of the crowd a clammy cloak that made it hard to breathe. Adriano pushed his way forward, ignoring the curious stares of the men and the appreciative looks of the ladies.

How the hell he was going to find her in this, he didn't know. Assuming Benedict had been telling the truth and she wasn't really at the movies or something. Any place safer than a bar.

But knowing Lil, she was likely to be here. At least if the Lil he'd seen in Vegas was the real deal.

He'd start at the bar and work his way to the dance floor. If she was at the bar, the sooner he could get her away, the better. If she was only dancing... Well, again, he had to get her out of here. The volume of the music couldn't be good for the baby. Didn't she know that the baby's ears were already working? She must, because he'd told her to start playing music for the baby.

Two passes of the bar didn't turn her up. More than one person gave him a dirty look as he shoved through the crowd—his scowl must have been ferocious.

All right, she wasn't at the bar then. Which eased his worry a hair. But she was still in here somewhere.

And then he heard it, through some miraculous pause in the music. Her laughter.

Adriano shouldn't have been able to hear it, not over the general noise, but he had. There, in that corner. That's where she was.

Her laughter rang out again, bright, happy, and then the music started up again, drowning her out. No matter. He knew where she was now.

He forced his way through the crowd, aiming for the spot where the laughter had come from. He couldn't see her, but he knew she was there. She had to be—no one laughed like she did. He pushed forward again, coming to some tables with groups clustered around them, everyone clutching a beer and shouting to be heard over the music.

He saw her then. Long hair flowing down her back, tight jeans molded to her ass and thighs, and her sweet mouth tipped up in a smile. And her belly—Jesus, when had that happened?

There was clearly a bump there, a not-so-gentle curve that came from more than simply a big meal.

She was showing.

He had to get her out of here. This was no place for a

pregnant woman. Someone could elbow her right in that belly of hers, and then what?

Time to collect her and take her home. But before he could get her attention, the man standing next to her sidled up close and hooked an arm around her waist.

What the fuck?

Instead of punching him in the balls, Lil smiled up at him, tilted her ear close to his mouth to catch what he was saying. Close enough for the man's lips to touch her skin if she moved even a millimeter.

Adriano knew this bar was too dangerous for Lil to be in, and he was going to show that son of bitch touching her just how dangerous.

LIL LEANED CLOSER TO BEAU, laughing at the story he was telling about one of the barn cats and how it had ended up terrorizing one of the bulls today.

God, but it was loud in here. She didn't remember the bar being this loud before. Maybe alcohol had a temporary deafening effect and since she wasn't drinking, the bar was louder than she remembered?

It also wasn't as much fun as she remembered. Oh, she had no desire to drink, and she was still having fun... but somehow it was muted. Or at least wasn't at the pitch she'd imagined when she was twirling Bea around the kitchen.

She really wouldn't mind going home if she was being completely honest. But she'd dragged her cousins out, so she couldn't leave early. Although her feet ached and she could already feel them swelling. A lovely side effect of pregnancy.

Beau was finishing up his story, which *was* pretty funny, so she set her hand on his arm, leaned in to tell him—

He was yanked away from her, quick enough to almost make her fall over. She caught herself and went to glare at the asshole who'd knocked over Beau. Who the hell was trying to pick a fight with him?

Adriano.

Her heart jumped and jerked like a startled rabbit. *Shit.* She had no idea he was coming back tonight. Not that she would have changed her plans or anything. Not for him.

"What the hell do you think you're doing?" he growled, his accent thick and rough as he shook Beau.

"Uh, Adriano?" Beau raised his hands. "It's me. It's Beau."

Adriano blinked, stared openmouthed at the other man, then blinked some more. "Beau? What are you doing here? And why are you touching my—how do you know Liliana?"

Time to step in. "He works for me, you idiot," she snapped. Screamed really, to be heard over the music. "Now let him go."

Adriano obeyed, his fists releasing even as his jaw tightened. "You go out drinking with your employees?"

"He's not here as my employee." Not that she owed him an explanation. "He's here as Penny's boyfriend."

Penny waved sheepishly from across the table.

"Penny?" Adriano put a knuckle to his forehead, then let his hand drop. As if Lil was giving him a headache with all this. Well, she hadn't invited him. This is what he got for barging in like a Neanderthal.

"Yes. Penny, my cousin." It was hard to put enough sarcasm in the words, shouting as she was, but she tried anyway. "And Beau is her boyfriend. But you already know him from the rodeo, don't you?"

"He doesn't know me," Bea put in. She held out her hand. "Professor Beatriz Schuler."

Oh, Bea did not like him. She only pulled that professor stuff when she wanted to intimidate someone. Although, Adriano *had* just tried to beat up Beau. Not a great first impression. If he threw this bar trip in her face, she could throw that in his.

Adriano shook her hand. "Pleased to meet you." He dropped Bea's hand and turned back to Lil. "You should not be here."

"Why?" Forget that she wasn't having that great a time, forget that she kind of wanted to go home—she was definitely staying now.

He wrapped his fingers around her upper arm. Not tight, but not loose. "This place is not for pregnant women."

She stared at his hand on her. "I'm not drinking." Every word a dart of warning. "So what's inappropriate?"

"Perhaps we could discuss this outside?" Even in the dim light, she could tell his face was darkening.

"Perhaps you could just send me an e-mail about it?" she asked as sweetly as she could, given that she was still shouting.

The song faded to an end, the overall volume of the bar dimming. His fingers didn't ease for a moment. She held his gaze, not a bit intimidated, as he held her arm. She wouldn't blink first. She'd never blink first.

"Liliana!" a somewhat familiar voice trilled. "Liliana Merrill, is that you?"

Shit. Of all the people to show up right now...

She turned, pulling her arm from Adriano's grasp. Luckily, he let her, or else she would have had to wrestle him in the middle of the bar to get free.

Just as she'd feared. Michelle MacPherson was coming straight for them.

"Michelle," she called back with just as much fake happiness. "Such a surprise to see you here!"

Lil wasn't lying about that. Michelle had three kids, two of them still in diapers. Lil was amazed she found the time to even leave the house. But Friday night at the Stampede was the best place to collect the latest gossip. The dirtier, the better for Michelle.

"You too." She looked Lil up and down. "I heard that you were expecting. Is it true?"

Judging by that look, Michelle damn well knew she was. Lil put on a fake smile. "Yep."

"Wow." Michelle's eyes went wide, all fake shock. "That's so surprising. You being a career girl and all." She made *career girl* sound like Lil was standing on a street corner.

Lil had known this would happen, that word would spread and some people would congratulate her and mean it while others would use it as a cover to jab at her. It was a small town, and she'd been here her entire life—she couldn't be friendly with everyone. It still sucked though.

"Well, things change." She couldn't keep the tightness out of her voice or her stance.

"But, honey," Michelle said, her voice dripping with concern, "you're not seeing anyone. You're not even married. Who's the father?"

Whoa. That was quite a bit more claw than Lil had been expecting. Did she go full bitch here or pretend that Michelle hadn't so sweetly insulted her?

"I am," Adriano said, his accent heavy.

He wrapped his arm around her shoulder, pulled her in close. His hold was warm, reassuring, but his expression was grim. Okay, maybe she didn't need to go full bitch, at least not yet. Not with Adriano stepping up to support her.

Michelle's smile slipped when she saw Adriano. "Oh. I don't think I've ever met you." She frowned. "But you do look familiar."

"You watch plenty of rodeo," Beau said. "This here's Adriano Silva. I'm sure you've seen him riding bulls."

Her mouth made a perfect *O*. "Really?" She looked Adriano up and down, a spark of envy in her eyes.

Oh, this reaction was delicious. Lil bit her bottom lip to keep from smirking. Maybe it wouldn't be so bad to have the story of her pregnancy traveling through town, not if the bit about a smoking-hot bull rider being the daddy was included too.

"Really," Adriano said dryly.

"Well, congratulations." Michelle sounded a bit stunned, no doubt knocked for a loop by Adriano's looks. "But should you be here? I mean, it's really not a good place for a pregnant woman."

Michelle couldn't take off without one last parting shot, could she? Pretty weak one though, considering she was still sneaking glances at Adriano.

"Don't worry," Lil said, "I think I'm smart enough not to accidentally pick up a beer."

"Well, you should head home, just to be safe." Poisonously chirpy.

Michelle was going to twist this story into Lil being three sheets to the wind, she already knew.

"But Michelle," she replied, just as chirpy, "if I'm dumb enough to accidentally drink beer, however will I have the brains to drive myself home?"

Adriano began to shake next to her, his body bumping

hers as he did. He was... *he was laughing*. Straight up jiggling with it.

She laughed too, because it really was ridiculous, trading veiled barbs with an acquaintance from high school and flaunting Adriano as some kind of conquest. But mostly because he was laughing and she couldn't help but laugh with him.

Michelle stared at them as if they'd gone crazy.

Adriano took a deep breath, continuing to laugh under his breath. "We're not here to drink," he told Michelle. "We're here to dance." He pulled Lil closer to him, gave her a scorching look. "Aren't we, darling?"

Damn. She'd only wanted to poke Michelle back a bit, but Adriano was getting out the big guns. She liked his style.

Why couldn't he be like this all the time? Funny, loose, still a little arrogant—he *was* a bull rider—but someone she actually wanted to be around.

She batted her eyelashes at him. "Yep, sugar pie."

He waggled his eyebrows, his lips twitching. "In fact, this is our song." It wasn't; the singer was belting out how much he loved his truck. Adriano tugged her toward the dance floor and away from Michelle. "Nice to meet you," he called over his shoulder.

Lil didn't even bother to look back at Michelle as Adriano led her away; her attention was all for him, the confident thrust of his legs as he walked, the nip of his waist, the tightness of his ass. When they hit the dance floor, he pulled her into his arms, closer than was really necessary. And man, could he dance, his hips swinging in a way that ought to be illegal.

"You know, I'm still mad at you," she said. Because she was. Even though he smelled sinfully good and felt like heaven pressed up close.

He leaned in, put his cheek against hers. "What?" He had to growl it into her ear to be heard over the music. She got the shivers anyway.

"I'm still mad at you." *Hold on to that. Don't let his sex-god status distract you.*

"I know."

When he didn't go on, she asked, "Don't you even care?" It sure sounded like he didn't.

"I do. But for right now, I want to dance with you. Who was that woman?"

"Oh, we went to high school together." She shrugged, because Michelle didn't concern her a bit. "We really didn't get along then and we don't get along now."

"What happened?"

"The usual high school stuff. She's harmless, really, and I wasn't always as nice as I could have been to her." Not that Lil had been a bitch exactly, but she'd been less likely to hold back when she was younger.

"Ah. Do you know everyone in town?"

What did he mean by that? Hard to tell when he was talking so close to her ear. Which continued to make her shiver. "Pretty much, since my family's been here forever. And now Michelle will tell everyone how she saw pregnant Liliana Merrill whooping it up at the bar. She won't actually say it was scandalous—she'll let her tone do that for her."

"What do you care what she thinks?"

"Usually I don't, but when you live in small town... You can pretend you don't care what people think. But at the end of the day it's only that. Pretending."

He didn't speak for several long moments. He kept moving her around the dance floor, still as graceful as before, but there was a tension there. She couldn't quite put her finger on it, but she sensed it anyway. He moved his mouth closer to her ear, the barest hint of stubble brushing along her cheek, the scent of him filling her senses.

"There's this guy on the circuit." Deliberate, measured. He was telling her something important here. Her fingers tightened on his shoulders, urged him on. "He always makes comments. Nothing too serious, just digs meant to get under your skin. And sometimes when he makes them, I pretend I don't understand."

There was a hint of shame, a dab of self-loathing there. If she turned her head just so, she could brush her lips across his cheek, tell him she understood and sympathized.

Instead, she said, "But you do understand. And it does get under your skin—his comments and pretending you don't know."

The same had happened to her when everyone had said she shouldn't be breeding bulls. She'd smiled and done as she pleased—but the barbs had remained embedded, no matter how she pretended they weren't.

"It does," he said. "Better that though than punching him in the face. Which would get me kicked off the circuit."

"Don't do that. Then I won't be able to brag about my handsome Brazilian bull rider baby daddy."

He laughed, spun her out and back again with easy grace. Man, he was killing her tonight with all the laughing and sharing of confidences. They should meet in a bar more often if he was going to act like this. She could fall in love with this Adriano Silva.

But he'd still leave for his home, taking their daughter with him and breaking Lil's heart.

She sighed and let her head droop a bit.

"Hey." He gave her a little shake. "No frowns on the dance floor."

She forced a smile, because it was nice to dance with

him. She ought to enjoy the moment while she could. "I thought you wanted to get out of here right away." She grinned at him. "But get you out on the dance floor and you can't seem to stop."

He shrugged. "I can't help but dance with a beautiful woman."

"Why, Mr. Silva, are you flirting with me?"

He spun her around, pulled her back in close, tucking their hips together. "No. Seducing you."

Whoa. Was she dizzy from the spin or from his confession? Maybe both. He was seducing her with movement, holding her so close, cheek-to-cheek, their bodies pressed together.

"What about our bargain?" Breathy, stunned. She couldn't pretend not to be knocked for a loop from that.

They'd agreed—*No sex.* Meant to not complicate matters, but things felt pretty damn complicated anyway.

"You're unhappy." Unhappiness twisted through his own voice. "I'm clearly failing on my end."

A lump formed in her throat. She couldn't deny it. It wasn't his job to make her happy, only to show her that he could care for the baby... But he *was* making her happy tonight, and she wanted it to go on. To keep this Adriano and send his evil e-mail twin away forever.

"I think we need to renegotiate," he said. The unhappiness was gone, replaced with rough heat.

Her entire body pulsed in response. "Yeah. We do." Oh God, she really, really wanted to. "But probably not in the middle of a dance floor." Common sense and all. It was one thing to have gossip about her pregnancy going around, but gossip about humping a dude in the middle of the Stampede was something else entirely.

"Perhaps we could renegotiate one key thing soon though?"

She knew exactly which one he meant. *Yes. Yes. Yes.*

"How about we work on that one tonight?" She turned her head, skin sliding against his, her lips brushing the tiniest of kisses on his earlobe. "In my bed."

Chapter 9

IN THE END, THERE WASN'T any negotiating about the no-sex clause. They silently agreed to drop it, which suited Lil just fine.

She and Adriano stumbled out of the Stampede with barely a wave to Bea, Penny, and Beau—although Lil did catch the shock on Bea's face—and raced for the truck. They kissed madly at stoplights, Lil cheering every red light and cursing every green. When they arrived home, they stumbled lust-drunk through the hall, hands and mouths and limbs tangled, tasting, exploring.

At the hallway he went left. She pulled him right.

"My room," she said. "It's this way." All breathless and dazed. She felt like he was still spinning her on the dance floor.

Lil ignored the mess in her room, unembarrassed by the clutter strewn through it. He wasn't here for the décor.

As if to prove her point, as soon as she shut the door he had her pinned to the wall, burying his face into her bare shoulder. She dragged her nails across his back as he rubbed his stubble across her neck. Fuck, but that was good.

He used his hips to pin hers against the wall, his hard cock rubbing against her sex. Her pussy flooded with heat, and she grabbed his face and kissed him with desperation. *Faster. Harder. I need you.*

He nipped at her bottom lip, sweet sting followed by the hot caress of his tongue. He slid a hand between her thighs and rubbed through her jeans. "Jesus." His fingers fluttered as if he were shuddering. "I can already feel how hot you are."

She clamped her thighs together and thrust herself against his hand, as shameless as a cat in heat. Too long, it had been too long without him. The pleasure was building crazy fast, draining the blood from her brain, making stars dance behind her eyes. "I can feel how hard you are too. Hurry. Let's hurry." She thought she might sob out this last: "I need you."

He eased the pressure of his body a fraction, lifting his head but keeping his hips tight against hers. He watched her for a long moment, a torturous moment.

"Faster," she urged again. "Harder."

Why wasn't he doing something? She knew he was as turned on as she was. Had he changed his mind?

Oh God, he couldn't leave her like this. Her brain would explode with this much lust clogging it.

He caught one of her wrists, then her other in the same hand. A sharp, sexy reminder of how large and strong his hands were. He dragged her imprisoned hands up over her head, held them there. She was spread and vulnerable for him, her breasts pushed forward even as his hips pushed hers back, putting a wanton curve into her back.

"No." He said it clearly and distinctly.

Shit. He had changed his mind. But why grab her like this?

"No," he said again. Softer this time. "Not fast. Slow." He drew the word out to double its usual length, and she shivered as it ran across her ears.

"I need you," she tried again. If he drew this out, kept her at this fever pitch for any length of time, her brain would melt.

"I need you too." He rubbed his cheek across hers but ducked out of the way when she tried to capture his mouth. "I want to tear you apart, it's been so long." His hand tightened on her wrists, a subtle warning. "But I'm in charge, and we go slow. Understand?"

Oh, that sounded scary hot. Would she even be able to survive what he had planned?

She nodded, unable to look away from the gold of his eyes. She'd been well and truly caught by the tiger, and now he was going to take his sweet time stripping every bit of pleasure from the marrow of her bones.

"Good," he said, as if she were a particularly bright pupil. "If I let you go, do you promise to do as I say? All of it, without hesitation?"

Oh boy. He wouldn't hurt her, but this domination stuff... they'd never done anything like it before. "Are you—?"

He laid a finger across her lips. "I would never hurt you. You're always safe with me. Trust me."

A new wrinkle. Mind games only then. It excited her, imagining what he might have planned. She nodded. "Yes. Master."

He laughed softly. "Don't overdo it. Besides, I like my name on your lips, especially when you're screaming it as you come."

Melting. She was going to be a puddle by the end of the night. A very happy puddle.

"I'm going to release you now. Remember: slow."

"Or what?"

His laugh was darkly amused. "Do you really want to find out?"

She did... and she didn't. Perhaps more on the *didn't* side. "Okay. I'll be good. Good and slow."

He unwrapped his hand from her wrists one finger at a time, never taking his gaze from hers. Time felt painfully, exquisitely stretched as he did. He had not been kidding about *slow*. This was positively agonizing.

She lowered her arms, peeped up at him through the veil of her lashes, all innocent obedience. "Where should I put my hands, Adriano?" She drew his name out as if she could fuck it with her tongue, enjoying the roll of the syllables through her mouth.

"Around my neck," he ordered quietly.

When she did, he scooped her up into his arms. Her body vibrated with lust, but something warm knotted in her stomach at his gesture. Romantic, protective, sheltering—this gesture was everything those e-mails hadn't been.

He laid her out on the bed, then leaned over her.

"What now?"

He tapped her on the hip, sending sparks dancing through her. "Slow," he reminded her. "I want to look at you." He ran a hand over the swell of her belly. "The baby is changing you."

Her body, not her. She was still the same. The reverence in his voice made her squirm beneath her skin.

Adriano didn't notice her discomfort. He stared at his hand splayed on her belly as if it were an old master painting. But it wasn't—it was his hand, her body, ordinary as ever. She lifted her hips, reminded him of what they were really doing here. And it wasn't making goo-goo eyes at her stomach.

His gaze snapped to hers, his eyes wide. Then they darkened.

Oh yes, he was getting back on track.

A smile tipped the corners of his mouth. "I told you slow." He slipped a hand under her shirt, lifting up to expose—"What the hell?"

He blinked down at the stretchy Lycra covering her bump. Heat flared in her cheeks, pounded in her ears as she snapped up and pulled her shirt back down. Stupid maternity jeans. She'd forgotten all about them. "I can't fit in any of my old clothes," she muttered.

He unpeeled her hands from the bottom of her shirt. She fought for half a second, then let him have his way.

"Did I tell you to do that?" he purred, as thick and soft as a jaguar's paw, barely hiding the claws beneath.

"No." Her skin prickled with delicious chills.

"I don't care what you're wearing. Because I'm going to have it off you in about two seconds."

Hell yes. "I thought you said slow?" She shouldn't taunt him, but the sooner they got to the naked and sweaty part, the sooner she could forget about him seeing the maternity jeans or the look on his face when he was touching her belly.

"Greedy," he accused her softly.

She shrugged because it was true.

"Be careful what you demand." His smile went feral. "You might not like it when you get it."

She didn't think that was true at all. Not when it involved what he could give her with his hands, mouth, body. Lowering herself to the bed, she tipped her head back, pushed her chest forward. Offered herself and her obedience.

"Good. That's better." He slipped off her T-shirt, her nipples tightening when the night air touched her bare skin. And even more when his gaze ran greedily along her. She reached back to unhook her bra—

"No. Leave it. I want you just in a bra and panties for now." He sounded like a man with a plan. A sexy plan.

She relaxed and waited for his next move. When his hands went to her waistband, she lifted her hips, helped him slide her jeans down her legs. Once she was down to her bra and panties, she lifted one knee, canted herself slightly toward him, and let him look his fill.

His breathing went slow and deep, his nostrils flaring with each inhale as his gaze ran across her for several long moments. The scraps of fabric covering her were hardly anything, yet she felt veiled from him, a thin, gauzy barrier separating him from her.

Did he sense that barrier too? Was that why he was simply looking?

She kept very still, wanting him to break this spell. This was his game, and his move should be the first.

He reached up, long, strong fingers spread wide, and set his hand on her breast. His thumb found her nipple and flicked, the caress muted by the fabric. He climbed onto the bed and straddled her, his denim-covered thighs rough against her while the silk of her bra was soft between her nipple and his thumb. He made no move to remove her bra, just kept up a steady rhythm at her breast that she should have found infuriating, it was so languid. Instead, she was lulled, entranced.

His free hand slipped between her thighs, found the folds of her sex, and traced her through her panties. Just as unhurried as his hand at her breast, both caresses hushed by the fabric left behind at his command.

She suddenly realized why he'd ordered her to leave on her underthings: the barrier stretched the sensation, spread it farther, rather than letting the sharp spike of pleasure hit hard. He'd said slow and this was how he was going to do it.

It was like sinking into the most perfect bath of pleasure, slipping inch by inch with each press and circle of his fingers. She'd never had a climax come on like this, as it crept in on quiet feet, surprising her with the intensity.

His thumb found her clit—deliberately, she was certain, as deliberate as everything else he was doing—and she sank several inches deeper at once. A shock to have the pleasure rise so quick and she gasped. He settled his thumb on the hood of her clit, broad and thick. And then he pressed. Millimeter by millimeter, each new increment making her pussy clench. Her panties began to grow damp, all of her slipping beneath the surface now.

She opened her mouth wide, pulling for air, urgency filling her lungs.

He took his hands away.

She took several sharp breaths, blinked hard as the drowning sensation persisted. God, he wasn't even touching her and she still couldn't breathe. "Please don't stop," she panted. "Please."

He wrenched aside the crotch of her panties, finally going fast, and lowered his mouth to her. When he sucked, she screamed. She wasn't sinking into an orgasm —she was falling, and fast, a cliff diver rushing toward the ocean.

When she hit the surface, her climax was as drawn out as the lead-up had been, leaving her panting and flushed and dazed for who knew how long.

Jesus fuck. Not even a real phrase, but her brain was scrambled. Totally scrambled.

"Lil?" Concerned and a touch scared. Adriano's brows pulled together as he set a hand on her shoulder. "Are you all right?"

"You weren't kidding about slow." A bit slurry since her lungs were still working double time.

His smile was pure triumph. "See what happens when you just listen to me?"

She'd give him this round for sure. The rest of it they could argue about tomorrow. "Can I move now?"

"Hmm. Why?"

"Because I want to touch you." Her fingertips were itching with the need.

"All right," he said, a king granting a royal favor. She went for his shirt and he caught her wrist. "But still slow. And I'm still in charge."

Yes, *very* kingly. "Oh? Maybe we should pick a safe word then." She wanted to puncture that imperial assurance with some teasing.

"Safe word? What is that?"

Huh. Safe word must not translate to Portuguese. "If you do anything I don't like, I say that word—something like *helicopter*—and you know to stop."

He raised an eyebrow. "You could also just say, 'Knock it the fuck off.'"

She laughed. "I guess that is more my style."

"So you don't like slow?" Disbelief made his words dry.

"I loved slow." She twisted her hand within his hold, caressed the iron fingers wrapped around her wrist. "I'm only teasing you." *In more ways than one.*

"I warned you about that." The tiger had returned.

"Oooh, is it time for my punishment? Remember you've got to stop when I say helicopter."

He laughed. "Of course. But you won't need it. We're going slow." Oh, he made it sound like such a threat, one that made her clench her teeth in anticipation.

He stripped off his shirt, the play of his muscles beneath his skin making her mouth go dry. He was so fucking cut, his hours of training written in the power of his limbs. His injuries were written on his skin as well. Her fingertips remembered the feel of those scars, wanted to feel them again.

His jeans and boxers went next. He was fully erect, his cock as proud and strong as he was.

She pulled a breath in hard through her nose. Since he was a bull rider, a person might suspect what lay beneath his snap-front shirts and Wranglers, but seeing all that lean, honed muscle in the nude... Her heart took a stutter step left, then right, dancing to the beat of her pulse.

"Like this, do you?" He fisted his cock, quite deliberately rubbing every inch, putting on a performance for her. And what a performance.

"Yes." That crazy pleasure was spiking again, stealing her voice.

"Greedy woman," he said with rough affection.

"Yes." The only word she could form, so she held her arms out to him.

He released himself, set one knee on the bed, braced himself with a hand—and stopped. "Do you have any condoms?"

"Yes. But... do we need them? We just got tested and, well—" She gestured to her stomach.

He bent his elbow a bit, came in closer. "I've never done that." His breath was warm, slightly spicy.

"Me either." Skin-to-skin with him. It frightened her a little, which was silly since he'd already gotten her pregnant. But they hadn't meant to do *that*—if they did *this*, they would mean it.

"If you want to, then I want to." His eyes had darkened to bronze. He clearly wanted to very much—but if she said no, he'd respect that.

Her stomach crept toward her throat. "Yes. I want to."

A weight settled between them, pressed the air from her lungs, made his movements languid, deliberate, as he lowered himself between her thighs. His cock pressed against her pussy, and although she knew it wasn't logical, she could feel the difference. She shifted her hips, made more room for him. Her gaze caught his, held. There was something open, almost raw in his expression. She felt her own expression open in response, almost as if this really was their first time and they were caught unaware of the awkward, fumbling intimacy of the act.

He reached between them, positioned himself, fingers brushing her sex. He gasped at the contact. "So wet," he muttered. "So wet."

She caught her bottom lip between her teeth. He would *feel* that wetness, that welcome her body had for him, just as she would *feel* him.

He pushed forward, a ragged breath leaving him. "Slow." More reminding himself than her.

Her hand found his shoulder, the other finding his cheek. And their gazes, still locked. She couldn't have looked away if she tried.

He pressed forward another inch. Delicious stretch, delightful pinch as she accommodated him. "So big," she whispered to him. "I can feel every inch."

His eyelids sank closed, his hips surging forward to give

her more. She lifted her own hips to meet his, welcoming him even deeper.

They held like that for a moment, his arms taut as they framed her, the tension in him vibrating under her palms, as joined as they ever could be. When he began to move, it was controlled, as if he was determined to wring every last sensation from this experience. For her part, they could do this forever—separating almost to breaking, then coming together as deeply as possible—over and over and over again.

His eyes opened, and the light within them pierced her heart. "Liliana." A groan, torn from between his teeth. Then several long phrases in Portuguese, things she couldn't translate but that sounded worshipful. Things she was certain he'd never said to her before.

Who was this careful reverence for? Her, Liliana, as a woman he desired? Or as a woman who was carrying his baby?

She shut her eyes tight. *No.* She'd take it for her and her alone. This was only sex. Sex like she'd never had before, but still just sex.

She opened her eyes, dug her nails into his back. *Faster. Harder.* How she'd thought she wanted it before, how she usually wanted it.

But he didn't oblige. He kept his steady pace, driving them both on at the tempo he wanted. And damn her body —it responded again with another of those crazy, drowning orgasms, a tidal wave of pleasure leaving her gasping and sputtering.

He came right along behind her, his cock jerking within her as he climaxed, an unfamiliar warmth spreading throughout her sex.

His come. He would pull out in a second but leave his

come behind. It seemed unspeakably dirty, a brand of his set inside her—but in a twisted way, she loved it.

He collapsed on top of her for a second, slick with sweat and his breath ragged in her ear, his weight another welcome mark on her. But then he rolled to his side, only his hand touching her arm.

"Are you all right?" he asked.

Honestly, she wasn't sure. It had been amazingly, incredibly hot—and amazingly, incredibly intimate. The heat she could handle. Growing closer to him, falling for him...

No. That was not happening here. She would not make the idiot mistake of assuming that sex without a condom meant true love.

"Great," she said. "Didn't even have to use my safe word."

A joke, but it fell like a lead balloon between them. He went stiff, then took his hand from her arm.

"Good. I'll... I'll let you sleep now. You need the rest." He pushed off the bed and began hunting for his clothes on the floor, his shoulders hunched.

She swallowed hard. That had been... that had been mean of her. She knew better. "Hey," she said. "You can sleep here. If you want."

A peace offering, one that left her vulnerable. He could say no, strike back at her.

But she hoped he would say yes.

He turned toward her, shirt in hand, still gloriously naked. But his expression was shuttered. Completely unreadable.

She held her breath.

"I won't disturb you?"

Not yes, not a no. "I'm a pretty restless sleeper. I'll probably end up kicking you."

He was still for another moment. Then he dropped the shirt. "Just say helicopter if you want me to leave."

She smiled and made room for him. "Sure thing."

He settled on the bed, not touching her. They lay like that for what seemed like forever, her skin aching at his nearness. Maybe she could reach over, make it look like an accident, and brush against him? She could try.

"Can I hold you?" His voice from the darkness, but nothing hesitant about it.

She didn't say anything, just slid into the circle of his arms. They both released a contented sigh at the same time.

"Go to sleep."

Another order from him. But one she was happy to obey.

Chapter 10

THE SUN'S RAYS WERE ALREADY chasing away the chill of the morning when Adriano made his way outside. Only six a.m., but it was already heating up. The day would be a scorcher even for late spring.

Spring in April. Adriano almost laughed. He hadn't quite gotten used to the switch in seasons up here. He'd never realized that for all that the temperatures were near the same, the heat of spring was very different from fall, at least not until the seasons had been reversed on him.

Not that he had to get used to these odd seasons. He'd be back home next year, and the seasons would return to where they should be.

A few years more. A few dollars more.

But his mantra wasn't as steadying as it once had been. He'd awoken at about three a.m., still on Colorado time. An extra hour to work out, to watch some videos—only he hadn't wanted to do any of that. He'd wanted to stay in bed with her, to hold her close. She was warm and soft and felt so right in his arms.

That was why he'd made himself get up.

This was how it would begin—the slip in focus, the shattering of his concentration. One morning of giving up on training would turn into two, then three—and then he'd find himself at the bottom of the rankings, wondering how he'd ended up there.

And where would his family be then? How would they pay for his mother's medical care?

They wouldn't, which was why he'd climbed out of bed.

He worked out for an hour, pushing himself harder than usual, welcoming the strain in his limbs, the burn deep in his muscles. He'd be sore come tomorrow. Then he checked in on Lil, who'd still been sleeping, curled around a pillow, her hair spread behind her. He'd wanted to climb back into bed with her—so he went to his room to shower instead. Afterward, he'd slipped out for walk, needing some fresh air and open space.

As for space, there was a lot of it, the ranch spreading as far as he could see. He passed the chicken coop about five minutes from the house. The chickens were clucking to each other as they scratched at the straw. A contented chicken made some of the nicest sounds in the world.

Rufio trotted at Adriano's heels, running ahead every so often to sniff at something interesting. He could almost imagine the dog was his and they were off to do their morning chores together. A dangerous fantasy.

But it all felt so right, walking on a cool morning through the open air, a faithful dog by his side, the livestock calling good morning, even though the landscape was all wrong. This was another thing he missed about home— simply walking the land, letting the wide, wild stretch of it strengthen him, revitalize him. He never had time any longer to be the *peão* he was in his bones. A man shouldn't spend too long away from the land—it scrambled his head.

But after next year, after he won a championship, he'd have all the time in the world to walk his land. And he wanted his daughter by his side as he did.

Adriano pushed on toward the barns in the distance where Lil was setting up her bull-breeding operation, separate from the other stock on the ranch. He wanted to see what she'd done, what kind of bulls she already had. He'd never thought much about the breeding side of it, at least not as much as Lil had, and he was curious.

He walked past the chickens, through an orchard with more kinds of fruit trees than he'd ever thought existed, past the goat pen, and he still wasn't even halfway there. The size of this place... it took up probably half this mountain valley, dwarfing even the casino he'd passed on the way in.

Although it wasn't quite as big as the ranch he'd grown up on. Estancias in Brazil tended to be in the thousands of hectares. As a boy, he'd wandered the estancia all day long and barely seen even a slice of it.

Once he was done with the rodeo circuit, he could buy a ranch this size back home. He'd raise his cattle and his family there. It was what he'd always dreamed of, his mother, brothers, and sisters all there, a place where he could care for and protect all of them.

But this situation with Lil—and not just the parts involving the baby—was complicating that dream. He'd meant to earn his money and leave America behind. But he couldn't do that if it meant leaving his child behind. And after last night, he wasn't so certain he wanted to leave Lil behind...

He turned at the crunch of gravel behind him.

Lil, dressed for the day, was coming along the path, her hands shoved into her pockets and her bump poking out before her. Rufio bounded over for a rub behind his ears.

"Morning," she called as she gave Rufio a pet.

He'd run early from the cozy sensations the sight of her had evoked. But she brought new ones with her now, ones that made him want to take her hand and walk over every acre, pretending it was theirs. "Morning." He kept all that he was feeling from his voice. "How did you sleep?"

She looked well enough, her green-gray eyes sparkling and her skin glowing in the pink of the sunrise. A man would be happy to wake up to that. Adriano certainly had been.

"Good. And you?"

"Fine. I didn't wake you up this morning, did I?" He didn't think he had, but it was polite to ask.

She shook her head. "I thought *I* got up early, but you've got me beat."

"I'm still a few hours ahead."

Rufio bounded back toward him, jumping up for more petting.

"Rufio, get down," Lil ordered.

He crouched down. "Don't scold him." He rubbed at the dog's ears and was rewarded with a happy doggy grunt. "What kind of dog is he?"

"I call him a Jack Russell terrier, but he's got something else in him. Maybe some cairn or fox terrier." She studied him, but he kept his gaze on the dog. "Did you have dogs growing up?"

"There were dogs all over the ranch. We could play with them, all the kids that lived there, but they weren't really ours. They were like this." He searched for the word in English, couldn't find it. "Not any one kind of dog."

"Mutts."

"Yes, that." For all that none of the dogs had belonged to him, there had been one that he'd been especially attached to—a brown brindle male that had slept on their front porch and had been his shadow most days. The dog had died the year he'd left for the rodeo circuit in Brazil.

He hadn't returned to the ranch for any length of time after that, and now that he'd moved his mother into her own home, there was no reason to return there. So why did the sight of this dog that wasn't even his make him feel so homesick for a place that wasn't his either?

He straightened up. That wasn't his dog. This wasn't his home. And Lil wasn't his woman.

They stared at each other for a long moment, all out of conversation. Or perhaps putting off what needed to be spoken of next.

Last night had been for release and selfishness. But today was for confronting what was wrong between them.

He took a deep breath. Here in the fresh start of a morning outdoors was the best place to do it. "I know you're mad at me," he began. But he wasn't certain why, so he left it there. She'd known he'd be gone a lot for competitions, he'd e-mailed while he was away, asking how she was and checking up on her—what was to be mad about?

"Clever of you to figure that out." She set her hands on her hips. "Was it me saying that exact thing last night that clued you in?"

He bit back his exasperation. At least most of it. "I can't reach out to you if you insist on sinking your teeth into my hand."

She narrowed her eyes. "You really see yourself as the victim here, don't you?"

The edge in her voice sharpened his own temper. "I sent you messages asking how you were and you replied with *bend yourself.*"

"No, I said *Get bent.* And you weren't asking how I was."

Her hands curled into fists. "You were trying to run my life via e-mail."

He'd only meant to ensure she was taking proper care of herself... but perhaps she hadn't seen them that way.

Focus. Concentration. Control. He tried so hard to cling to those things with her, but he always failed. First in Vegas, then last night.

Given her reaction to his e-mails, maybe it was better to let some control slip from his grasp.

"I didn't mean them that way." A bitter thing to swallow down, that he might have been wrong. But they had to get along for the baby's sake. "I only wanted to take care of you, even when I couldn't be with you."

"It didn't feel like caring. It felt controlling." But her fists uncurled, became hands again.

All right. The messages *had* been a mistake. "Perhaps next time you can tell me that instead of telling me to get bent?" he asked gently.

Her chin dropped a fraction. "Yeah. Maybe that wasn't the best thing to say."

Not quite an apology, but some progress. He'd take it. "I'll do better with the e-mails."

She sucked in a breath. "This bargain thing... it's just not going to work."

His heart smacked hard against his ribs. She was going to call in the lawyers. He'd already lost. "I..." But he had nothing to save his cause.

"You aren't ever going to believe it's better that the baby live with me," she said. "And I'm never going to be happy with the baby gone so far for so long. Our ties to our families—they're too strong and too far apart for us to ever come up with a good solution."

But her expression wasn't as hopeless as her words.

"Then what do we do?" He, who always had a plan, a detailed accounting of how to get what he wanted—he had no idea what to do here.

"You're not leaving for at least a year, right? And we... Well, last night..."

Her cheeks were turning pink, which was an odd look on such a brash woman.

"Do you regret it?" He cocked his head, studying her expression. If she regretted it...

"God, no!" Her eyes went wide. "It's just... Where do we stand now?"

She sounded as confused as he was. They had crossed a bridge last night, make no mistake. But where they were now, he couldn't say. And she couldn't either.

He pondered that. "Ignoring our attraction clearly doesn't work."

"Clearly." Dryly teasing.

He suppressed his smile. "But we had agreed before— sleeping together was a bad idea."

It still was a bad idea—he might fall for her. And if he did, he'd be torn between the piece of his heart she held and the one he'd left behind in Brazil. A dangerous risk to take.

But resisting her... it seemed he could do anything but that.

"Honestly?" she asked. "I liked you last night." As if she didn't usually like him. "Dancing, sleeping together... I liked *us* last night."

He felt exactly the same way. He'd enjoyed himself more than he had—well, since Vegas. But his impulse to stay with her this morning, to forget working out, to set aside his focus just for a day... He had to fight that if he was going to keep sleeping with her.

A few years more, a few dollars more.

A warning to himself now.

But she deserved the truth. "It was the same for me," he admitted.

She took a sharp breath. "How about this? We go on like this, like we were last night. And when you're ready to leave"—her voice caught—"we'll reassess things then."

He lifted a hand to her face, wanting to touch the tinge of pink in her cheeks, to see if it was as soft as it looked. "Everything will change when the baby comes." What he meant was: *I'm still leaving. Nothing's changing that.*

She understood. The resigned set of her mouth told him that. "Yes. But let's see where we are then."

He tilted his face closer to hers, wanting to taste her lips. "I'm still going to take care of you. You're the mother of my baby. But better than I have been."

"No more e-mails?" Soft. Not at all accusing. He guessed she was thinking more of kissing him than those messages.

"No," he said. "I'll call you, and you can smack me over the phone when I'm annoying you."

She smiled. By God, what a beautiful smile she had. "You can tell me when I'm being too snappish."

He kissed her then, because he couldn't hold back any longer. Her lips were slightly cold from the morning air, but they quickly warmed beneath his. He slipped a hand into her hair, pulled her closer.

Her mouth opened, her tongue caressing his. Bold, so bold, this woman. She lit a fire in his blood like no other. His hand tightened in her hair, and she moaned with pleasure.

Not too far. He couldn't strip her naked here, with the goats looking on. Tonight. Tonight there would be time enough for everything he wanted to do. He eased his grip, pulled his mouth from hers.

She blinked and bit her bottom lip, now a deeper shade of rose from their kiss. "Can we just forget the chores?"

She meant it as a joke, but it hit deeper than she could have suspected. Because he could forget a lot of things with her, things he mustn't forget.

He forced a smile. "Your chickens will miss you."

She grabbed his hand. "The chickens can wait. I want you to see the bulls."

He took in their surroundings as they walked, the rolling mountains enclosing the valley, the low scrub creeping all around. It wasn't ugly exactly, but it certainly wasn't as pleasing to his eyes as the grasslands of his youth. Too brown, too low, too... barren.

"It's not much like Brazil, is it?" As if she could read his mind. Or perhaps only his expression.

"No." Here the plants clung to the mountains almost desperately, as if just one dry season away from dying completely. At home, the plant life was so exuberant and green. Not quiet like this chaparral. "Have you ever been to Mato Grosso do Sul?"

She shook her head. "No. I've never even been to Brazil."

If she'd never been, she had no idea of what she was missing. Of what their child would miss if she stayed here in California. "You'll have to visit sometime," he said, careful to keep his tone casual. "It's a very beautiful place."

"It's beautiful here too," she said.

He didn't argue, although he didn't quite see the beauty she did. "Did you always want to run the family ranch?"

She shrugged. "It wasn't a question of wanting. I just knew this was what I would do. Even when I went to college, I only wanted to get back here, to where I was born." She took a deep breath, looked to the sun peeping over the peaks to the east. "This place, these mountains—they're in my blood. They're the marrow at the center of my bones."

"I feel the same way about my home."

After that, they walked on in silence—what was left to say after that mapping of how far apart they were? So they kept quiet as they made their way to the barns.

Even half-finished, the entire spread was impressive. The finished barn already had three bulls in it, and another barn was under construction. A few other bulls were out to pasture—well away from each other—while the arena and chutes sat empty. Everything had been planned for maximum orderliness and efficiency. And sturdiness. That was important with bulls.

Adriano couldn't think of a single thing he'd have done differently. Once she got it completely up and running, this operation was going to be something. He propped himself against the arena fence rail and studied the chutes. "What else needs to be done?"

"Well, we've finally got the remote dummy set up, and the cameras should be ready to go next week."

The remote dummy was a weighted robot that was strapped to a bull's back. When the bull bucked the way you wanted him to, you punched the remote to launch the dummy off his back, making the bull think his clever move had thrown his rider. One of the few ways to train a bull.

The cameras were to record a bull's rides. The videos were the bull's calling cards, his chance to be picked for the top events. The higher the bull's scores, the more cowboys he threw, the more famous he became. Some bulls were more famous than the riders.

"It's very impressive," he said. A little disconcerting to look at all this and realize she was trying to create a bull better able to put him into the dirt. A great bull made for a great ride, but some bulls were practically unridable. Those were crowd favorites. Lil would probably breed more than a few of those bulls here over the coming years.

"Yeah." But she didn't sound quite as enthusiastic as before, her shoulders drooping as she looked over her work.

"Are there problems?" he asked. Perhaps too personal, but Lil would simply tell him so. He could always count on bluntness with her.

She clasped her elbows. "A few. But nothing I can't handle." Her usual bravado was hollowed out though.

"Is there anything I can help with?" But he didn't know about breeding the bulls—he only rode them. Another thought occurred to him. "You're not training them in the chutes or flanking them yourself, are you?"

She slid him a cool look. "No. Beau's doing all that now."

Thank God. But he didn't say it aloud. Best not to shatter the mood between them.

"The other problems are only people being dumb about a woman raising bucking bulls." Lil pushed off from the fence, clearly done with her confessions. "Let me show you the lab."

"Lab?"

She led him to the half-finished barn, to a set of rooms there. She wasn't joking about it being a lab. There were microscopes and petri dishes and other things he couldn't name. All of it neat and orderly to the point of obsession. He kept to the doorway, not wanting to get dust on any of it.

"Here's where we'll do the IVF and embryo transfers," she was saying, gesturing to the benches and equipment. "I'm hoping once we get things running, we can offer those services to other stock contractors."

"How do the IVF and embryo transfers work?" He had a

general idea, but this looked much more involved than he'd imagined.

"Well, they ship the bull's semen to us in liquid nitrogen."

He nodded. He'd seen a collection being made once, which might have been the most surreal experience in his life, involving a bull mounting a dummy cow.

"In the lab, we use that sperm to fertilize an egg taken from a cow," she went on. "After that, we implant the embryo into a different cow."

"So the bull and the cow never meet and the cow never meets the calf?" That might be more surreal than the semen collection.

She grinned. "Romantic, huh?"

It was fascinating. So much technology involved in something so primal. "Can I see it happen sometime?"

"Sure." Her phone rang then. She frowned at the screen. "Hang on. I've got to get this."

She went out the door, muttered something to whoever was on the other end, then disappeared around the corner.

Who was she talking to? Curiosity burned in his gut, but he stayed where he was.

She might be the mother of his child, they might be sleeping together—but he had no right to know. Which was a separate burn, apart from the curiosity.

He kept his eyes on the lab, away from her, and tried hard not to listen.

LIL GLANCED BACK at Adriano as she put the phone to her ear. Not that he would necessarily listen in, but she already knew he'd be the topic of this particular conversation.

"Hi, Bea." Lil's face was already hot, and all she'd done was greet her cousin. "You're calling early."

"Don't remind me. I have the worst headache this morning." Her cousin's voice was pretty brisk for someone who had a splitting headache.

"Maybe you should be sleeping it off." *And not calling about what I know you're calling about.*

"Ha. I had to find out what happened last night."

Lil snuck a glance at Adriano. It didn't look like he was listening, but she went around the corner anyway. He *really* should not hear this conversation. "Um, we went home."

Bea sighed. "I know that. But with how you two were acting on the dance floor, what happened when you got home?"

"I don't think I can tell you all the details." She *knew* she couldn't tell Bea all the details. Not if she wanted to be able to look her cousin in the eye.

"So you made up?"

Made up, made out, had the most insane orgasm of my life. "I guess you could say so." Her voice had an odd flutter that she tried to squash.

"Should I start planning the wedding too then?" Bea asked dryly. Her cousin was already planning the baby shower—and that joke was *not* funny.

"Cute. We're just seeing how things go." She tried for light and easy but only sounded strained.

Of course Bea picked up on that. "How things go until he leaves the country, right?"

Lil set a hand to her forehead. It was way too early in the morning for this. She hadn't even had her one cup of coffee. "Bea, I love you. Dearly. But I'm not ready to talk about this."

"Okay." There was a scritching noise, as if Bea was

marking something off on a sheet of paper. "Did you do the baby registry yet?"

"The shower is months away!"

"And you'll keep putting it off until it's too late. Which is why I'm reminding you. I want to finalize the invitations soon, and I can't do that without the registry information."

"You are so anal," Lil said. Only Bea would want to finalize details on a party three months in advance. People planned surgeries with less precision.

"Yep." More scritching. Her cousin was definitely writing on something.

"Does that cover your checklist for this phone call?" Lil grinned.

"What? Uh, no, there's no checklist." But the scritching continued. "Well, that's about it. I'll talk to you later."

Lil shook her head as she hung up. *Don't ever change, Bea.*

It was way too soon to set up the registry, crazy soon even... but it was a Saturday. And she and Adriano were both here. Maybe picking out baby stuff together would help with the *getting along* stuff. Although if the baby went back with him, all that stuff would be useless, a harsh reminder of everything she'd lost...

Lil shook that off. No sense crying over something that might not even happen.

"Hey," she called as she made her way back to him.

He was still in the doorway of the lab. When he turned to face her, his expression was shuttered. As if he hadn't been thinking very happy thoughts.

"Is everything all right?" he asked.

"Oh yeah. Bea"—*wants to know what happened last night* —"was bugging me about the baby registry." She cocked her head. "I don't suppose you want to go pick out baby stuff today?"

"The baby won't be here for months." He looked a little horrified.

That was probably a *no* for him then. "I know, but Bea is very anal."

"Anal?" Now he really looked horrified. That definitely wasn't translating well to Portuguese.

"Anal retentive. It's Freudian." Explaining Freud was only going to make it worse, so she left it at that.

"Freudian. Okay." Confusion replaced the horror on his face.

"You know what? Let's not talk about Bea or Freud or being anal retentive. Let's go look at some baby stuff. And let people buy it for us."

He laughed, as she'd meant him to. "Okay."

So after breakfast—where she only had one cup of coffee, like a good girl—they headed out to the baby superstore. When they arrived and walked through the doors, it was—

"Whoa." Lil blinked. And blinked some more.

Overwhelming didn't even begin to describe it. Aisles and aisles of baby stuff, stacked all the way to the ceiling. Happy babies smiled out from boxes of diapers, playpens, and formula. And the clothes... racks and rack of fluffy, pastel tidbits.

God help them.

"I thought a baby just needed diapers," Adriano said, as fearful as she felt.

Lil had thought this would be a lark—not like setting up base camp at the Mount Everest of Baby Gear.

"A crib," she said faintly. Not that she saw cribs. "I'm pretty sure we need one of those."

"Okay, a crib and diapers."

They both remained rooted in place. She wanted to

reach for his hand, which was silly, because it was only a baby store—but the size of it was scary. This was what it took to keep a baby alive. All this.

An older lady with a kind face and a name tag came up to greet them. "Do you need any help?"

"Um, a registry?" Lil didn't mean to sound so confused, but dammit, the immensity of this place was scrambling her brain.

"Starting a registry? Or shopping off one?"

"Starting one." She could answer that with some confidence at least.

"Great. Let's get your info!"

The clerk motioned them over to a computer and began to take their entire life history. Or at least what felt like it. The sex, the baby's name—which they didn't have yet—the colors of the nursery, whether they were doing attachment parenting or not, breast or bottle feeding...

When they were finished, Lil was more than a little stunned. The clerk handed her a scanner. "Whatever you want on the registry," the woman said, "point the scanner at the barcode and it will be automatically added. Neat, huh?" She beamed at them.

"Yeah," Lil said uncertainly. After all that, they still had to go through the entire store? She took a deep breath. People had climbed Everest before—surely she could survive a baby store.

She glanced at Adriano, who'd been very quiet throughout the interrogation. "Ready?"

He didn't look ready, but he nodded.

They went back to where they'd started, facing down all those aisles, both of them in a gunfighter's stance. Lil held the scanner loosely by her thigh.

"We can do this," she said.

He took the scanner from her. "Of course we can. We work with bulls for a living." He raised his arm, angled the scanner toward the ceiling like a shooter who'd just drilled his target. "Let's do this."

"Right." His confidence was catching. "To the diapers."

They went through diapers—cloth and disposable—like a couple of pros, then picked out the crib in five minutes. But when they got to the bottles, the arguing started.

"A package of formula and some bottles isn't going to ruin the baby for breast-feeding," Lil insisted.

Adriano's jaw was set, the skin tight across the line of it. "The book says you shouldn't have formula around if you want to breast-feed. You might be tempted to use it."

That fucking book. That was it—*the Book* was going into the wood chipper.

"It's formula, not heroin." She stabbed her fingers into her forehead and imagined poking them into Adriano Silva's arrogant, stubborn fat head.

"The book—"

She held up a hand. "Stop. Stop before I lose it."

Praise all the saints: he shut up. She took a deep breath. They couldn't get into a fight here. She'd have to change tactics.

"Okay. Imagine this: there's a disaster." He made a disbelieving face, but she kept on. "I can't get to the baby, and you have nothing to feed her. Because I've got these"—she gestured to her chest—"and you don't."

His lips twitched. Was he actually going to laugh?

"So if we don't buy any formula, she'll have nothing to eat should something terrible happen. Or we could get one case, promise to never use it barring an emergency, and avert tragedy."

He was definitely trying not to laugh, his chest shaking

with the effort to hold it in. It looked like some well-timed jokes could soothe his temper just fine.

"You make an excellent point," he said dryly. "Let's get one case."

She smiled to herself as she hit the formula case with the scanner. This registry business was going to be easy.

Facing down the bedding tripped up the both of them though.

She could have a drawn a line down the shelves, blue and football and dogs on one side and pink and unicorns and princesses on the other.

"Wow," she breathed. "How can we pick something when we were not sure if it's a boy or girl?"

There didn't seem to be anything cute that didn't scream boy or girl. This bedding demanded that you pick a side in the gender wars—there was no middle ground. Lil pitied any parent who chose not to take advantage of technology and found out the baby's sex the old-fashioned way at the time God had intended.

"The doctor said it was probably a girl," Adriano said. But he didn't sound as certain as the doctor had.

"Probably. Not definitely." What if they got everything in pink and ruffles and it turned out to be a boy and he hated them forever? Or if they did have a girl but she hated pink and adored trucks? Gender wasn't destiny. And hell, their kid would probably end up resenting them when it was a teenager anyway.

Lil tapped the scanner against her thigh. It was a crazy train of thought, but here in this wonderland of baby crap, crazy thoughts seemed to be the only way to keep sane.

"It will be a girl." Adriano was certain now. "And we'll name her Gabriela."

He sounded like an oracle. So convinced, so definite.

Gabriela. Her daughter, Gabriela. Lil put a hand to her belly. *Gabriela.*

It was a good name. Lil could see herself saying that with love for the rest of her life. And occasionally with exasperation and annoyance. If the baby stayed with her.

And if the baby was with him, he'd do the same.

Stop obsessing over it. These circular thoughts would get her nowhere.

"Yes," she said, because he was right. She knew it somehow, deep within her. "Gabriela. Now where is the horse stuff? Because any kid of ours is going to love those."

When they were done with the bedding, they went on to the play pens, then the bouncy seats, strollers—Jesus, some of those were more expensive than a crib—bottles and Binkies, and finally, the clothes.

Lil had never been one to coo over baby clothes before, but something stole over her when she saw all the tiny little scraps of fabric, so soft, all pastel.

Her child would wear these. She'd have to place tiny limbs into those clothes, would cover an itty-bitty bald head with those hats.

It seemed almost impossible.

Adriano was inspecting a pair of pants that had "Cutie" plastered across the butt, with kitten-faces for the footies. "Did you ever see anything so adorable?" he demanded.

She hit it with the scanner. "Can you imagine how cute it will be on her? Our brains will probably melt."

"I found some other things she'll need." He took the scanner from her and began hitting all kinds of clothes. Most of them frilly and fancy and more appropriate for church.

The clothes were adorable, but so was he. "She'll need

some play clothes too," Lil pointed out, a laugh tickling at her lips.

"You're right." He added some Onesies and pants that wouldn't be too much worse for the wear with some spit-up on them.

Here they were, talking about the baby as if she were a real person and getting along beautifully. If they kept this up, maybe by the time he was ready to go back home, they could...

Could what? For all their talk of getting along for the baby's sake, neither one of them had ever mentioned marriage. *Don't jump ahead here. Take the days as they come.*

This was worse than obsessing over who was getting the baby.

Adriano continued to wildly tag clothes for the registry. If he kept this up, the entire girls' clothing section was going to be on there.

She set a hand on his arm. "I think that's enough."

He blinked as if coming out of a spell. "Yes," he said slowly. "You're right. What's next?"

She checked her phone. Good Lord, they'd been there three hours already. Exhaustion hit her in a sudden wave. But they weren't quite done. "Car seats. They won't let us leave the hospital without a car seat."

Picking a crib had been easy. The bedding issue got sorted once they decided they were having a girl. The clothes had been just plain fun. The car seat... picking a car seat was downright nerve-racking.

"Do you think the 'Safe-T Baby' side-impact protection is best?" she asked. "What's the difference between that and the 'Secure Ride' supplemental restraint system?" She read the information again, but that was no help. "And does a car seat really need drink holders?"

Adriano shook his head as if defeated. "I don't know. I just don't know."

They'd made it this far through the baby store, only to be vanquished by the car seats. Her head slumped. The baby superstore had won.

But they had to get a car seat. Out of all this, that was the only thing they *had* to get.

She stared at the Safe-T Baby seat, sized it up. "You know," she said, "you ride bulls, which is about the most dangerous thing a person can do. And all you wear is a protective vest. Maybe a helmet too."

He raised an eyebrow.

She gestured to the seats. "We don't even need any of this. Put a tiny little Kevlar vest on her, pop on a helmet, and strap her in. She'll be just fine."

His lips twitched.

"Don't laugh," she said. "Don't you dare encourage me. This is serious business, and I'm not being serious."

That did it. He busted out a belly laugh, then snatched her up and spun her around, kissing her right in the middle of the store. "You're right," he said. "Forget the car seat. Where can we find a protective vest in a newborn's size?"

She laughed now herself. "Can you even imagine a tiny baby in boots and jeans and a little vest? God, it would be the most adorable thing ever."

He set her down but kept his arms around her. "Adorable enough for us to take her out of the hospital without a car seat?"

"Probably not." She cocked her head, studied him. He was gorgeous when he laughed, his mouth stretched wide in a smile, his limbs lean and loose with pleasure. "Do you trust me?"

His expression sobered. "Yes." Simple. Direct.

She lifted the scanner, hit one of the car seats. "There. Done."

"Good choice." Still serious.

God, that felt good, to have him be easy in this. To not struggle over something involving the baby. They should do this more often, this not-fighting thing. "Let's turn in this scanner and get lunch. I'm starving."

He looped an arm over her shoulder, pulled her close, as if they were any other set of parents in the store.

Don't get too comfortable, Liliana. He'll break your heart when he leaves. Especially if he takes your daughter with him.

She pushed the thought away. They were happy, they were united. She wasn't going to let her better sense ruin that right now.

Chapter 11

DOMESTICITY HAD ITS VIRTUES, Liliana had decided.

They'd done the baby registry, gotten lunch, and then gone home so she could nap. Not something she usually did, but she'd wanted to try it out today. Picking baby stuff was more exhausting than she'd expected. Or maybe this pregnancy was finally catching up with her. At any rate, she'd gone to lie down, thankful that Adriano hadn't thrown her kindergartener crack back in her face, and slept for three hours.

When she woke up, feeling as fresh as new-folded laundry, they'd taken a walk around the ranch, this time to where the stock horses were kept. Rufio kept them company, and they were as sedate as any other boring married couple. But it had still been nice. After, she'd made dinner and they'd eaten on TV trays while watching a cutting-horse futurity.

Boring. Stable. Practically married. But somehow it was fun when she did it with him. Which boded well for their future, whatever that might be.

There'd been no sign of Luke—she guessed her brother

was giving the house a wide berth while Adriano was there —so it was almost like they *were* married and enjoying their alone time. It was nice. Better than nice—it was comfortable. Cozy.

They were doing the dishes together, her washing and him drying. Like any other married couple on a Saturday night.

"What do you want to do tonight?" she asked. They could go out, but after last night at the Stampede, she didn't feel much like repeating the experience. Not for a while. But watching TV didn't sound appealing. Maybe they could go to the movies. What kind of movies did he even like? Maybe something with a lot of action and explosions and fast cars. Or maybe not. Maybe he got enough of an adrenaline rush when he climbed onto a bull's back and didn't need a vicarious one.

"I know exactly what we're doing tonight." His confidence might have read as arrogance if she didn't find him so damned attractive.

"Really?" She guessed it wasn't getting naked and sweaty. They'd get to that later she was certain, but it sounded like he had something else in mind.

"I'm going to teach you how to dance."

"I already know how to dance." She handed him the last plate. "Remember what we did last night?"

"Yes. But you need to learn how to dance *properly*."

Okay, now he was slipping toward arrogance.

"I dance just fine!" He hadn't been complaining last night. In fact, he hadn't been able to keep his hands off her.

He shook his head. "You dance like an American. Pretty good for an American, but still like an American."

She should probably be offended by that on behalf of

her countrymen. She tried out some indignation. "How does a person dance like an American?"

He made jerky, marionette motions, a gruesome smile stretching his lips.

That was plain ridiculous. "I do not look like that." Surely not. Someone would have taken pity and told her.

His face relaxed and he bit his lip as he continued his puppet dance. He looked so completely silly she couldn't help but laugh.

"I—" She was laughing too hard to finish. "Did I really look like that?" she asked when she caught some air.

"Not that bad. But you do need to learn how to dance like a Brazilian. And I'm going to teach you."

Ooh, that sounded sexy. She could get behind that. It definitely sounded better than watching TV.

"Okay." She set her hands on her hips. "Show me how you dance. *Properly.*"

He gave her a slow, panty-melting smile. *Uh-oh.* "We should move into the living room. More space there."

And a couch, in case they felt the need to get horizontal at any point.

Once they were in the living room, he cued up some music on his phone.

She frowned. "What is this?"

"It's *sertanejo.* Brazilian country."

Portuguese still sounded so odd to her ears. She kept waiting for it to coalesce into Spanish, but it insisted on slipping into something more like French. Or maybe Italian. And the music didn't really sound like country, at least not American country. It was more like pop music. Although, a lot of American country sounded like pop music to some people.

"Come here," he ordered, pointing to a spot in front of him, his tiger eyes glowing.

She went to where he'd indicated, waiting for him to make a move. He took her in his arms, but sadly not too close.

"Okay, like this." He pulled her close and began to move to the rhythm, his hips swinging with it. An American dude wouldn't be caught dead moving his hips like that, but it looked so flipping hot when Adriano did it. She was mesmerized by his hips, by the way—

"Keep up," he snapped.

"Sorry." She tried to move in an approximation of his steps, but she was a beat behind him and couldn't catch up. "I was distracted."

He raised an eyebrow. "Eyes up here."

She giggled. "Stop flaunting yourself at me and I'll stop looking."

"It's not flaunting." His lips pursed prissily, his attempt to play the prude. It was cute. "It's dancing."

They kept at it for two more songs, trying to find the rhythm of the steps. Or rather, she was trying to find the rhythm. Adriano knew what he was doing, but he led so aggressively—he pushed her where he wanted her to go, his arms stiff and strong, his legs thrusting into her space, his hands tight on hers. Tight with frustration.

Instinctively, she pushed back, leaning into him, her back rigid, her jaw set. She wasn't going to blindly go wherever, no matter what the steps were.

When the song finished, he dropped her hands.

"What are you doing?" he demanded. "Move with me." He stepped forward to grab her again.

She stepped back. "You're pushing me. Ease up."

"You won't go where you should. What else can I do?"

That was unfair. She didn't know what she was doing here, and he expected her to do everything he was—and do it backward besides.

"You know, you might know how to dance," she said, "but I'm not certain you've figured out this leading stuff."

"You certainly don't know how to follow." As if she should be blindly and happily doing everything he decreed.

"No, I've never been a follower." If he wanted that, he should have slept with some other girl in Vegas and gotten *her* pregnant. "You need to *ask* me to follow you, not demand."

"You need to trust where I'm taking you," he said. Was this a dance lesson or a reflection of their relationship? "Listen to my hips and hands—don't fight them."

She'd done that once before and look where they'd ended up. Maybe she should just call off this dance lesson. There was no point if they were going to fight.

That's exactly the point.

She took in a sharp breath. The little devil on her shoulder was right: they had to get through this without fighting. This was a dress rehearsal for the big decisions to come. They'd managed the baby store; they could manage this.

She swallowed her pique. She'd make an overture here, in the interest of goodwill. "Can you slow down? I don't know the steps." She gentled her voice, let the frustration and stiffness leave her stance.

His expression softened. "Sorry. Sometimes I'm not a very good teacher. Don't worry about the steps. Listen to my body and yours and the music."

He pulled her close to him with just a hint of dominance. He wanted her between his legs, and he put her there. But his grip was gentle, his hands callused. Of course they would be—he spent a fair amount of time clinging to a bull's back with a rope.

They moved together, slower than they should, hesitant, and she could sense in him the urge to go faster, to be fluid. But she wouldn't have been able to keep up.

So they went slow and stumbling, their focus deadly serious on each other. Because this had become more than a dance—it was a chance to figure things out.

Their baby was depending on them.

Their steps clashed less, came together more. They still weren't truly dancing, but she wasn't behind him on the steps so much. She was getting it. Slowly, but she was.

He started to direct her more forcefully, his muscles tensing, pushing harder. She tensed, ready to push back.

They held like that for half a moment, winding up.

It wasn't going to work. They couldn't do it. She held her breath, waiting for them to explode again, to break apart.

Then, as if by some hidden cue, they both relaxed. *Listen.*

So she did. Not to the tension in his limbs, which was seeping away. But rather at the little, quiet things beneath. The pressure of his palm against hers, the angle of his hips, the flicker of his gaze.

They turned together, their bodies finding a common rhythm.

The song playing was a slower one—a love song. The music seemed to direct the both of them, deciding how they would move together. He wasn't leading, she wasn't following—they were under the spell of the melody.

His eyes held hers, his expression intent. She was caught in that golden gaze, the movement of his body holding hers even beyond the clasp of his hands.

They were doing it. They were dancing together.

He smiled at her, a wide, dazzling stretch. She smiled back, feeling the triumph in the edges of it. And the happiness filling the middle.

The song slowed and faded into silence. They smiled at each other for two more heartbeats, and then they were kissing, slow and happy at first, sharing their delight in what they'd done.

As it always did, the kiss turned hot, fierce, needy. She clasped his face, pulled him greedily to her. His hands at her hips were just as greedy, just as forceful.

She ground her pelvis into his, needing the friction there. The couch was so close—only two steps and she could have him over her. Two more seconds and she could have him inside her—

A truck door slammed outside.

She gasped, pulled away. Either Luke or Benedict. They needed to get out of here. She could feel his erection pressing into her thigh—he wasn't fit to be seen. And she didn't want to be seen.

"Come on." She grabbed his hand. The dance lesson was over, but the rest of the night had just begun. "Let's go to bed."

ADRIANO DIDN'T THINK he'd ever gotten ready for bed with a woman before. Brushing his teeth, stripping off his clothes, watching her get into her pajamas—he didn't wear them—it was an eeriness just under his skin. Not really uncomfortable, simply unfamiliar.

He lifted the sheets for her and she slid in next to him, her back to him and her gaze never meeting his.

They breathed into the dark for a time, waiting together.

Did she want him to touch her? Somehow, he didn't want to ask. This entire situation felt very married, and a husband didn't always have to ask with his voice. Sometimes he knew his wife so well he could ask with a touch. Could see in the subtle signs of how she brushed her hair, how she glanced at him as she pulled on her nightgown, exactly what she wanted.

Adriano wasn't quite there with Lil yet—might never be, depending on how things went—but he did want the chance to ask her with a touch. He reached out to her, settled his hand on the dip of her waist, right under her ribcage. Her nightshirt was thin from years of wear, soft from hundreds of washings. Nothing about it could be called sexy. Except she was clearly comfortable in it. And comfortable with him seeing her in it.

That wasn't sexy—that was *intimate*.

When his hand touched her, she went still for half a heartbeat, then twisted a fraction toward him. *Come find me.*

A husband would recognize that as an opening salvo. Not a *yes*, but a *convince me*.

He slid his hand forward, wrapped an arm around her, and tugged her toward him. She bent her head, lengthening the line of her neck. *Here's a spot you can kiss. To start.*

He lowered his mouth to her neck, breathed kisses at the juncture of her shoulders, along the steps of her spine, at the silken skin behind her ear. *Convinced?*

She wriggled her ass against his hips. *Getting there.*

He splayed his fingers and inched them down her belly, over the swell there, and found the end of her nightshirt riding her upper thighs. His fingertips brushed over the bare skin, waited for her legs to open to him. A husband would know exactly how long it would take before she surrendered in this game, having played it many times before.

This being new to Adriano, he could only guess. Two more strokes? Three more? He kissed her neck, using his tongue to caress as well, while still asking with his fingertips. *Convinced yet?*

She kept her thighs shut, her sex hidden from him. *Keep going.*

He opened his mouth on the tendon running from her shoulder to her neck, dragged his teeth across it. *There you go.*

She moaned deep in her throat, her legs opening. *There you go.*

Oh yes. His fingers found her folds, already damp. She'd liked this game of convincing. He stroked there for long moments, simply enjoying the wet, sleek feel of her against his fingertips. A husband might do this as well, without the intention of pushing her to a fever pitch—merely to relearn the body he already knew so thoroughly.

She wriggled her hips, catching his cock in the cleft of her ass. *I'm convinced. Let's go.*

He smiled to himself as he slid his knee between her thighs, opening her even farther. His other arm slid under her, anchoring her for his entry. It would be tricky, fucking her from this angle, but he wanted to stay curled around her like this, all of her enclosed by him. He angled her upper leg, shifted his own position—then drove home.

She gave a surprised, pleased grunt, which felt almost as good as the wet heat of her gripping his cock so tightly. He grabbed her hip, drove forward again. Another grunt from her, followed by a long exhale.

He thrust again and again, savoring the novelty of this angle, taking some pleasure for himself. When he sensed his climax building, he slowed, his fingers finding her clit. Enough of him taking. Time to give.

A long moan, higher pitched than before, came from her. A husband would recognize that noise, would know that it meant she was close. Adriano rhythmically circled her clit in time with his thrusts, dancing with her just as they had earlier. Another moan, even higher.

"Yes," he growled into her ear, "tell me how much you fucking like this." A husband might hesitate the first time to say such a thing to his wife, might wonder if she'd like it or be offended.

But Adriano wasn't her husband. He growled it without shame into her ear as his thrusts grew more rapid, more wild. A deep thrum started in the base of his spine.

She only moaned again in response, so he fucked her harder, spreading her legs wider, opening even more of her to him.

Close. He was so close. But she had to come first.

"Lil." A growl. A plea. "Lil."

She put her hand over his, working away at her clit. He stilled his fingers, then pressed hard. She liked that, the weight against her most sensitive spot. He didn't need to be her husband to have learned that. Her hips flexed urgently, forcing him to keep up with her, and all of her pulsed as she came.

Finally. Her pussy shuddered around his cock, pushing him toward his own climax. He came a second later, hips pistoning as he spilled within her, his thoughts nothing but a smear of pleasure plastered across his closed eyelids.

He held her close for long moments, still joined, both of them panting.

A husband would appreciate this afterglow just as much

as he had the first time. It wouldn't lose any of its charm with repeat experiences.

Adriano wasn't certain if he wanted to be a husband—not if it meant never returning home—but he did want to experience this with Lil again.

She was breathing fast, her back brushing against his chest with each inhale.

"Are you all right?" he asked. Her breathing was beginning to worry him.

"Yes." Soft and a touching wondering. "That was... whew."

He buried his face in her neck, breathed deeply of her scent. He had slipped out of her at some point, but he remained curved around her, most of her pressed against him.

Sleep beckoned at the edges of his brain, made his eyelids droop and his thoughts transparent. But one pressed forward, pushed itself toward his tongue.

Before he slipped completely into dreams, it slipped out: "Come with me."

"With you? Where?" Her own words were heavy with drowsiness.

"To my next competition. Come with me." He didn't want to be apart from her, not even for a few days.

This was how it began, the loss of focus, of purpose, that he feared. Needing her and giving in to that need like this. But too late. He couldn't even summon his mantra to remind him of why he shouldn't ask her this. All he could think was: *It's just this once. And I don't want to leave her.*

"When is it?" she asked.

"In three weeks." Crazy of him to ask her after being back for only a day. Who knew if they would even be getting along in three weeks, after all that time in each other's pockets?

Crazy of him to expect her to say yes right away, with no hesitation. Crazy of him to be disappointed that she hadn't.

"Okay." Her agreement was sleep drunk. But she had agreed.

"Good." He rubbed his face in her hair, taking in her scent as she breathed contentedly.

Would she remember in the morning?

Would he?

If they both did, it was meant to be. He closed his eyes, let the worry slip from him. And for the first time in a long time, Adriano let fate decide for him.

Chapter 12

SHARING A ROOM AT A RODEO–THIS was a novel experience for Lil.

She set her bag on the bed and looked around as Adriano shut the door behind him. One king-size bed. They better not get into a fight or the sleeping situation would get hairy.

Not that it was likely. The past three weeks together, her working, him training, dance lessons in the evening, sharing breakfast and dinner and a bed—heck, even the flight here —everything had been great. They'd laughed over the baby-shower invitations Bea had sent, debated more stuff for the baby—did she really need a high chair right from the get-go?—and spent some time going over bucking-bull stats. Beau knew his stuff, but Adriano's perspective was just different enough to be valuable.

She liked working with him. And maybe he liked working with her. Maybe enough to think about staying. Maybe.

Her fingers tightened on the handle of her bag, her knuckles going white. A big maybe. He still had a family and a sick mother back home. No amount of getting along would change that.

And it had only been a few weeks of working together and living together. She shouldn't make the mistake of thinking that was enough to change his course.

But this was their first rodeo as a couple. Which was what they were now. A baby on the way, living together, traveling together—what else could they call it?

Yet the concept made her a touch uneasy. Or maybe she was uneasy about the fact that they hadn't talked about what was happening. Couldn't say how long their coupledom would last.

She took a deep breath, released the handle of her bag. Day by day. That was how they'd agreed to take this. She turned to him as he came toward her. He tossed his bag next to hers, then pulled her in for a kiss. "Remember the last time we were in a hotel room together?"

She certainly did. The evidence of it was a big lump between them. "Want to try out the bed?" They didn't have anywhere to be, and his mention of the last time in a hotel room was stirring some very hot memories.

"I would." He kissed her again, then pulled away with a low groan. "But we have to feed you first."

For all that they'd been getting along, he was still pretty bossy. He meant well, but man, could he bark orders when he wanted to. She flopped down on the bed. "I know better than to argue."

"You're learning," he said with mock wonder. "I never thought it possible."

Bossy and funny. Although she liked his jokes better than his orders. "You're lucky you're so good in bed. Otherwise I'd never put up with your smart mouth."

He set one knee on the bed and leaned over her. "You didn't call it smart last night. In fact, you said—"

She laid a hand across his mouth. "That's enough out of you." If he kept going like that, she was going to have to tear his clothes off. And when he'd mentioned food, she'd discovered she was hungry. "Where do you want to eat?"

He nipped at her palm, and she snatched her hand back. "There's a Brazilian restaurant here we usually go to."

We. He must mean the other Brazilians. "Is that like an Argentinian steak house?"

He snorted. "It's much better. You don't mind eating with the other guys, do you? Most of them don't speak much English."

"My Portuguese is getting better." The dance lessons had included some language lessons too. She was picking up the dance quicker than Portuguese though, no matter how similar it was to Spanish.

"Yes, *hello* and *how are you?* will get you far." He was teasing, but there was a flicker of unease deep in his amber eyes. This was important to him, even though he was playing it off as casual.

She lifted a hand to his cheek. "Of course I want to meet them. They're your friends."

He had worked at fitting into her life—and now she would do the same for him. And happily so.

In the end, the language barrier wasn't so bad. A few of the other riders greeted her in English, and Adriano translated Miguel Barros's greeting—she had the sense Adriano looked up to him—but the rest of it was all Portuguese, stories and jokes and laughter spinning throughout the entire meal.

The service was similar to Argentinian barbecue, with

grilled meat carved tableside, but the food was quite differ-ent. There were chicken hearts (she passed on those), grilled pineapple (which she loved), and something called *aipim*, which looked like french fries. And everyone was very excited when a cut of meat called *picanha* was brought to the table.

Adriano leaned into her ear. "You can't find this here, not easily. You'll like it."

She did. She loved it—and not just the food. She loved how relaxed and happy Adriano was.

He was chattering away in Portuguese, a permanent smile on his face, most of his attention focused on everyone else. But his arm was slung around her shoulders, holding her tight to him, and every bit of food on her plate he'd given to her, not letting her dish anything out herself.

Before she'd met him, she'd have thought that kind of behavior weird, controlling—and she'd have run for the hills. But with him, surrounded by his friends and his brand of comfort food, she realized he wasn't trying to control her. He was *sharing* this with her. This was a tiny slice of his homeland that he wanted her to enjoy.

So she sat back, ate what he put in front of her, let the unintelligible conversation wash over her, and simply watched him. His shoulders loose and relaxed. His white teeth flashing as he laughed. His eyes warmed to the luster of new gold as they gleamed with amusement. His arm heavy across her shoulders, anchoring her.

She realized then why he had to return to Mato Grosso do Sul—really, truly realized it, deep in her gut. Nowhere else had she seen him look happier. He was content enough with her back in Cabrillo, but here, among other Brazilians, he was at home.

She pushed her plate away, the realization beginning to curdle in her belly.

She couldn't keep the baby with her, not if it meant Gabriela didn't get to see her father like this. Because this was Adriano at his very best. Gabriela deserved the very best.

Lil rubbed at her eyes, breathed through the weight of that decision.

She'd have summers with her daughter and maybe one day Gabriela would want to stay in America. Her stomach turned over. That would hurt Adriano so badly, having his daughter choose to leave him.

"You okay?" Adriano put his mouth near her ear, his breath warm, the concern in his voice vibrating against her skin.

"Yeah." She cleared her throat, blinked away the stinging in her eyes. "Just full."

Just half in love with you.

Idiot. She was an idiot. She'd known the score going into this, and it wasn't like she'd never see him again—they were going to have a kid together. She'd see him occasionally at least.

But it would make her happy to see him more than occasionally. She'd be ecstatic to have him here with her more permanently. Working with her on training the bulls. Teaching her how to dance. Raising their daughter together on her family's ranch.

But he would be heartbroken at losing that connection with his homeland.

She sighed, stared at her plate. So there they were. Back where they'd started. Except her feelings ran deeper now. And it would hurt worse when he left.

"Hey." He grabbed her hand, ran his thumb across her knuckles. "Are you sure you're okay? We can leave if you don't feel well."

She took a deep breath, put on as good a smile as she could manage. "Nope. Fine."

He smiled, not that he'd ever really stopped since they got here. "Want to try out your dance lessons?"

She pushed her sadness away. He was still here now and he wanted to dance. She'd enjoy today and worry about tomorrow when it came. Day by day—that was their agreement. "Sure."

He pulled her to her feet. "Only for a couple of songs. We need to be getting to bed soon."

There was nothing lascivious there, which meant he was thinking about being rested for his ride tomorrow.

When they arrived at the dance floor, Adriano pulled her close into a slow, sexy dance, crooning along to some *sertanejo* she didn't recognize. He had a lovely voice, deep and rich. She closed her eyes, the better to savor his voice and his body moving her with the music.

"Did you have fun?" he asked. A little wistful, as if he was worried she might say no.

"Yeah. Everyone was great." He didn't have anything to worry about—even with the language barrier, she'd enjoyed herself, if only to see him happy, so at home in his skin.

His hand tightened on her waist. "I should have translated more."

"No, honestly, I had a good time." She looked up at him, so handsome, so serious now. "I liked all your friends." She dropped her gaze, his expression too much for her at the moment. "You're really comfortable with them." Her voice caught on that last, even as she steered it toward steadiness.

He was quiet for long moments as he led her through the dance. "I'm comfortable with *you*."

She closed her eyes for a brief second. "Not like you are with them."

He knew it too—she could hear it in the way he'd said he was comfortable with her.

"I hope not quite the same." A tease from him.

But she didn't smile. When the song ended she said, "I'm tired and you've got a big day tomorrow. Can we just head back?"

She had the sudden urge to be alone with him, to have him completely to herself, his focus entirely on her. Selfish, yes, but if she couldn't have him for as long as she wanted, she'd be grabby while she could.

When they got back to the hotel room, they readied for bed together. Their usual routine, only in a different place. Funny how quickly they'd fallen into this pattern. She'd miss it when he left.

They crawled into bed together, and he curled around her. Her gut cramped at the thought of sleeping alone again. She'd more than miss this—it would kill her to say good-bye to him. But he was with her now and she was going to take the time she'd been given. She rolled over, took his face in her hands, lowered her mouth—

"Lil." He wrapped a hand around her arm, moved his mouth out of her reach. "I have to ride tomorrow." Regretful. But firm.

The air hissing from her deflated ego had to be audible even to him. "Yeah. You're right. Sorry, I forgot."

He hadn't put those kinds of restrictions on them in Vegas. So what was different now? And why was she letting it hurt so much?

She rolled away from him and curled deeper around her belly. It was all right. This was their deal.

He set a hand on her shoulder. But nothing more.

She lay there for long hours, staring into the darkness, his hand never moving from its perch on her shoulder.

ADRIANO WAS in his own world. His own head.

Lil could see that the instant he'd woken up. He'd hardly spoken to her from the moment they'd climbed out of bed, and even his demand that she eat breakfast was halfhearted.

She nursed her only cup of coffee for the day and watched him, her own plate already clean. Her appetite, which had been good before, was almost ravenous now. If she wasn't nibbling something every fifteen minutes, her stomach got put out and let her know it.

He'd left half of his own breakfast when usually he had the appetite of Rufio set loose in a ham shop. His gaze was fixed on the food left on his plate, but she didn't think that was what he was seeing. Not with that thousand-yard stare of his.

He was touching his thumb to each of his fingers in turn —forefinger, middle, ring, pinkie, then all over again.

Maybe he was meditating. Maybe he was praying, counting off the decades on his fingers.

Whatever he was doing, he was far away from here and her. Probably already on the back of a bull, at least in his mind.

"Ready?" She set her coffee mug down. She didn't need to be greedy for his attention just now. He was going to risk his life later today—he should do whatever was needed to prep for that. "I've got a meeting with Bob Stanton in fifteen minutes. Let's see if he sells us some of those cows we were looking at."

Bob had been weirdly noncommittal about selling her the cows when she'd e-mailed him two weeks ago. When she found he'd be here and Adriano wanted her to come anyway... well, it was the perfect opportunity to hammer things out face-to-face.

Bob was an old friend of her dad's, so he'd probably sell her the cows. But he also thought Lil had no business raising bucking bulls. And then there was the issue of her clearly visible bump... She heaved a sigh. She still hadn't heard back from the rodeo committee, so she was due for some good news here, right?

Adriano nodded absently to tell her he was ready, but when she reached for her wallet to pay, he glared as he went for his own. Maybe he wasn't quite as inattentive as she'd thought.

They made their way to the arena where some cowboys were putting the finishing touches on the chutes. She waved to people she knew, Adriano waved to others, and then they were at the gate that led behind the chutes. She couldn't go past that gate—from here on, they'd have to go their separate ways.

Stop being so melodramatic. You'll see him again in a few hours.

"Well, good luck," she said, shoving her hands into her back pockets to keep from reaching out for him.

He stared at her for a long moment, then glanced around them as if checking to see who was watching. Finally, he pulled her into his arms. Not for anything lustful —just to hold her tight.

She held him back just as tight, her belly between them. *Be safe. Come back to us.*

When he released her, she wasn't ready to let him go. But she had to. She watched him disappear behind the gate, her tongue between her teeth so that she didn't call after him and draw attention to them.

Besides, she had a meeting to go to. They both had work to do here.

BOB STANTON HAD LOST MOST of the hair on his head and added quite a bit more padding to his belly, but mostly he was exactly as he'd been since Lil was a kid—brash, with a loud laugh and a punishing handshake.

"Lil." He somberly shook her hand this time, still with too much force. But he didn't pull her in for a hug.

Uh-oh. That was bad.

"Mr. Stanton." Best to start from a position of youthful respect, applying to her elder for help. "It's great to see you. How are Mrs. Stanton and Donny?"

"They're fine." He looked worried. And a touch uncomfortable. "How are your mom and dad?"

"They're great." She forced herself to be cheerful. "They said to say hi. They'll be in Tulsa this year in July and hope to see you there."

"Yeah." But he didn't sound enthusiastic about it.

Okay. If he didn't want to chat, they could get down to business. "About those cows I e-mailed you about—"

He held up a hand and shook his head. "I can't sell you those cows."

Shit. "Why not? Did someone else snatch them up first?" Joking, light, and not at all as anxious as she was feeling.

"That's not it. I heard about"—his gaze flicked to her stomach—"about you and that bull rider."

Heat crept into her cheeks. "Yep. Adriano and I are expecting a little girl in a few months here." She waited for him to offer his congratulations, which would have been the polite thing to do.

It didn't come. "Your dad is one of my oldest friends. We grew up rodeoing together." He drew a deep breath, as if trying to soothe a sour stomach. "So it kills me to say this, but: I think you're screwing up your life, Lil."

She caught her angry response between her front teeth. He was her dad's friend—he'd known her forever. She couldn't spit her anger at him, so she reached for something more placating. "I'm asking you to sell me a few cows. Not approve of everything I do." Her tone wasn't as friendly as before, but not as mad as she felt.

Bob shook his head. "That's the thing. You shouldn't be raising bulls at all. I didn't say anything because of your dad." He had, actually, but she let it slide. "And you... Well, I've heard about what you get up to at these events." The burn in her cheeks flared with new heat. "I can't condone what you're doing, having a baby like this."

It's not yours to condone. Unbelievable that a man she'd known her entire life, a man who claimed to be friends with her father, was trying to slut-shame her. She could rattle off a dozen indiscretions of others in the rodeo world—Hank Smith's third wife, who'd once been the babysitter; Julie Johnston and Jim Ferrell's decade-long affair, well-hidden from their spouses but no one else; and then there was Scott Black's pretty serious cocaine habit. She didn't see Bob scolding any of them.

All she could see was Bob's face twisted with discomfort, his gaze angled away from hers, his shoulders hunched. He wasn't enjoying this at all. He wasn't finding any triumph in telling her how immoral he thought she was.

She took a deep breath. No, she couldn't snap at him.

Sometimes I pretend I can't understand what he's saying. That's what Adriano did when that other guy strained his temper to the breaking point.

She wished she could do that right now, just shrug and sidle away, pretending that the shame and awkwardness wasn't real. But that wasn't possible. She could, however, compromise.

"I'm very sorry you feel that way," she said quietly. "But I understand why you think you can't sell me those cows."

Surprise dissolved some of the discomfort on Bob's face.

"Regardless of what you think of me," she went on, "you couldn't find a better father for this baby than Adriano. It might have been an accident that put us in this situation, but it was a happy one for me and our little girl."

It was true—Adriano would be a wonderful dad. Stricter than most, but he'd laugh a lot too. And teach his children how to work on a ranch and dance.

But he'd only do those things for one child of hers.

She took a shaky breath, willed herself to be strong. "If you'll excuse me then." She didn't know where she'd go—there were a few hours before the bull riding started—but she had to get away.

"Well..." For a moment Bob looked like he might apologize. But he only said, "Thank you for being so understanding."

She nodded in response, her voice no longer strong enough to hold her words. She went back to the hotel, cried in their room for a bit, using one of Adriano's shirts to dab at her tears. For the first time since she'd decided to breed bulls, she began to believe that it might not work. That she might fail at it, and not because her bulls weren't good enough. Just because of how the rodeo world worked. And it hurt.

But not as badly as her decision about the baby. It was the right one—she knew it because she ached so badly. Adriano would love their daughter, raise her to be a wonderful person—and Lil would stay here to face the ruin of her bull-breeding dreams, the disappointment of her family, and her own loneliness. But she would survive if not thrive.

She cried all that out into Adriano's shirt. Releasing those tears felt good. She'd never enjoyed crying before, but this pregnant crying was different. Relieving.

Once she was done, she washed her face, reapplied her makeup, and headed back to the arena. She had some bull riders to watch—or maybe just one in particular.

Adriano would be up near the end of the first round, so she had about an hour of anxious waiting to get through. The crowd was keyed up, roaring with each and every ride, but the noise and excitement only made her own nervousness that much sharper. She made sure to sit by herself, far away from anyone who knew her. She couldn't handle small talk right now.

She'd seen him ride before in Vegas. And in videos. She'd appreciated his skill then, been smug that she was sleeping with the man who rode a bull like he did.

But this time was different. This time felt real and painful and terrifying in a way it hadn't before. She set a hand on her belly and shifted on the metal bench, her hips protesting at the uncomfortable seat. Of course he would be fine. He did this for a living. As dangerous as the sport was, there were plenty of retired bull riders, happily shuffling off to a ripe old age.

It would be fine. He would be fine. Although, if this were a bad movie, this would be where he was injured almost to the point of dying. As he recovered, he'd have an epiphany about the meaning of family and how little bull riding meant in the scheme of things.

This wasn't the movies. They weren't guaranteed a

happy ending no matter how good things were between them.

Chill out, Liliana. Everything will be fine.

Then the announcer boomed, "Adriano Silva." His name bounced through the arena, and her fragile composure shattered. Her gut twisted as he climbed into the chute, his body tense, his expression tight.

Oh God, he was really going to climb onto that bull and she was really going to watch him.

There was a flutter, deep in her belly. The baby. *Gabriela.* She set her hands over her belly, took a deep breath. She had to remember to breathe. For the baby.

"That's your daddy out there," she whispered. Kind of silly, to whisper like that, but it also helped ease some of her anxiety and just felt... good. Like Gabriela was real, and Lil's feelings for Adriano were real, and they could make this thing work.

And maybe all those things could be true.

Adriano was poised on the fence, readying himself to climb on the bull. His hat hid his face, but the rest of him was electric in his focus, body still and yet crackling with suppressed energy. She wondered if he even knew anything existed beyond that bull and that chute at the moment.

He settled himself on the bull, checked and checked again his grip on his rope. And checked once more.

She stopped breathing.

There was a long, quiet moment—the bull calm in the chute, Adriano's head bent, his hand on the gate, as if both were gathering themselves for what was to come.

Then Adriano nodded and the gate swung open.

Her breath hissed from her teeth, every muscle in her tensing. She was rigid, fearful—but Adriano wasn't any of that. He was fluid, not ahead of the bull, not behind it—man and animal were moving together. Almost like a dance.

A violent dance, one that could leave Adriano crippled or dead if he made a misstep, but some of the tight panic left her as wonder took its place—because this was one hell of a ride. A fucking amazing ride.

He only had to survive it.

Eyes wide on him, she counted off in her head: *One. Two. Three. Four. Five. Six. Seven. Eight.*

No horn sounded. *Where was the damn horn?* This ride was over. He had to get off.

And yet she didn't want it to end, it was so perfect.

A long, startling blast made her jump, had her snapping off the seat.

The horn. That was the horn. She let her breath slide between her teeth, caught it again. He still had to dismount.

This was most the dangerous moment of all. The crowd was roaring, mouths open wide, feet stomping, hyped up. *Shut up,* she wanted to tell them. *It's not over yet.*

Instead, she put all her focus on Adriano, willing him off and safe. *Don't get hung up. Don't get hung up.* A prayer to him, to the bull, to God—to whomever would listen and get him clear of that bull.

The bull jerked to a hard stop. Adriano came off.

On the wrong side.

Now. If his hand was coming free, it should be now.

The rope never released. His hand never came loose. He was trapped against the bull.

OhGodohGodohGod—he's hung up. She put her knuckles to her mouth, bit until copper sparked on her tongue.

The bull fighters were moving in, trying to slow the bull, to capture his attention long enough for Adriano to get his arm over the bull's back and get his hand free of the rope.

The roar of the crowd had dimmed, transforming into a low groan rising from thousands of throats.

Lil bit deeper into her hand, giving the pain as an offering for his safety. And she realized then, with her breath stopped, her heart stilled, and her teeth sunk deep into her own flesh, she'd give anything for him.

This was a hell of a time for her to realize she loved him.

Shorty, one of the bull fighters, darted in and smacked the bull in the middle of the face. Jesus, he was quick. The bull stopped for half a second, shook his head as if Shorty's smack had been as small as a fly landing.

That was all the time Adriano needed. Slick as shit, he had his arm over and his hand out from under the rope.

Sour and sharp, the breath she'd been holding left her lungs, blowing past her fist still clamped in her teeth.

Jesus, she was biting herself. She lowered her shaking hand to her side, all of her sagging with relief, set it on her belly, on the child they'd made together.

Thank you. Thank you. He was safe. She loved him. She bowed her head, sank back onto the bench, curled both hands around her belly. "He's okay," she whispered to Gabriela.

Everyone around her was cheering as Adriano walked safely away, the bull having run out of the arena with no further problems.

It had worked. She'd bitten herself, which was crazy, but it had worked. He was safe. She began to shake, starting with her insides and vibrating out to the very tips of her fingers. She wasn't sure she could watch another ride of his. This was horrible, the fear and anxiety, and God, it had been such a good ride. A great ride.

Adriano stopped by the fence, closed his hand into a fist

and kissed it, looking heavenward. That thanks had been for God.

Then he took off his hat and tossed it into the crowd, which went wild. He knew exactly how beautiful that ride had been. That thanks had been for the crowd.

Did he see her? Did he have anything for her?

He started to search the crowd, his smile dissolving, his brow knit.

She was sitting down. He couldn't see her.

She jumped back up, waving wildly. She didn't care who saw her like this, just as long as Adriano saw her.

Their eyes met, his smile returned, and she gave him one back.

He took his gloved hand, that hand that had been clinging to the bull, brought it to his lips... and tossed her a kiss.

Or perhaps he tossed it to Gabriela. Or perhaps the both of them. Which was as it should be.

It didn't matter. She loved him. She loved their baby... Hell, with Adriano safe and blowing her kisses in front of everyone, she felt like she loved everyone.

When he was finished, once the final round was over and he'd maybe won the whole thing, she'd tell him how she felt. Tell him everything and see how they might make this American-Brazilian thing work out.

Not only for the baby, but for the both of them.

Chapter 13

ADRIANO SHOOK OUT HIS HANDS as he made his way past the chutes and toward the locker rooms. Adrenaline and anxiety churned together in his gut.

It had been a hell of a ride. The best of his career. And he'd done it with her watching.

He closed his hand into a fist, the burn in his palm stinging as he did. He'd gotten hung up with her watching too. The fear on her face... He closed his eyes. A hell of a thing to see right after the best ride of his life.

So he'd blown her a kiss, a kiss to wipe away that fear. A kiss to tell her how he felt.

Away from her, he rode like shit, his concentration shattered.

Here, with her close at hand, his focus was total, his ride a... He shook his head, still not quite believing it. He prayed he'd have another ride like that before he died.

He stopped at the locker-room door, forced his hand to unclench. He unfastened his vest. He'd forgotten about that, so keyed up had he been.

No more. He had to calm down. He shrugged out of his vest, pushed open the door, calm, collected.

They all congratulated him as he entered, slapping his back, American *and* Brazilian, the entire room united in admiration for his ride. He let it wash over him, accepted the warmth that seeped through the chill of his calm.

He'd earned this.

As it faded, each cowboy returning to his own group of friends or simply his own thoughts, Adriano turned toward the circle of his countrymen. It had been a great ride, but it wasn't over yet.

"Thought Brazilians didn't get hung up."

Adriano froze midturn. *Fucking Crane.*

He clenched his fist, imagined sending it into Crane's smirking mouth. "Happens to everyone." He kept his voice neutral, free of his agitation. Trust Crane to try to rile him right now.

"Course, you got hung up on the biggest prize of all, didn't you?" Crane's smile curdled.

Adriano jaw clenched. *Pretend you don't understand, that you don't know he means Lil.* His arm ached with the urge to strike Crane. "It was just one ride." *One hell of a ride.* "I haven't won this thing yet." A shrug, which did nothing to release the frustration building in him.

"I saw Lil out there."

Fuck, if Crane wasn't going to let this drop... *Nothing. You'll do nothing.* "Yeah. She's here with me." Adriano lifted his chin, let some of his anger show. Maybe that would get Crane to back off.

"Is she?"

There had been an edge to Crane's question that made Adriano's hair rise. "Yeah. She is." *She's mine. So fuck off.* He took a step toward Crane. Forget pretending he didn't understand—he was going to make Crane understand that Lil was taken.

"Well, usually when she's at an event, she's not with someone." Crane let his smile drop, all pretense of friendliness gone. "Usually she's *looking* for someone."

So that was his game—Adriano wasn't falling for it. "Not anymore." He went to sleep beside her every night; that was his baby in her belly—Crane's innuendo couldn't compete with that.

Crane put back on his smile, tipped with vicious triumph this time. "Well, that's a damn shame because she was a good lay."

The air seemed to hiss out of the room. There was a release in the atmosphere surrounding them all, as if Adriano now knew what everyone else had. The other men were relieved—and charged with chilled anticipation at Adriano's reaction.

It was true then. She *had* slept with Crane.

Adriano blew out the sick feeling from that, forced his thoughts to white blankness. *Pretend you don't understand.* But he couldn't fake it, not anymore, not with this.

He couldn't think about who else she might have slept with—that was in the past. She was carrying his baby. They were joined forever by that. He had to focus on that.

Where was his focus? All he could see was Crane's leer.

"She didn't tell you?" Crane raised his eyebrows mockingly. "Huh. Well, congratulations, man." The fucker held out his hand—actually *held out his hand.* "Getting a girl that rich pregnant—she's got billions. You're fucking set for life now, thanks to your sugar mama." He laughed. "*Mama.* Yeah, you caught her good and tight."

Adriano stared at Crane's hand, shoved into the space between them. Then he lowered his head and charged, exactly like the bulls they rode. He caught Crane in the belly with his shoulder, wrapped his arms around the other man, and drove him into the wall.

Crane met the cinder block with a satisfying grunt, so Adriano smashed his shoulder into Crane's belly again, pinning the man between his strength and the unyielding bricks. Another grunt.

Adriano could do that all night, just slam that son of a bitch against the wall until his shoulder ached and Crane's ribs cracked. But two hits—one for him, one for Lil—was enough.

He let go of Crane and the man sank to the floor.

Wait. There was one more thing.

Adriano sent his fist into Crane's jaw, snapping the back of the other man's head into the wall. A wet, fleshy *crack* echoed throughout the room.

That was for Gabriela.

Adriano stepped back, his chest heaving, and took in what he'd done. Crane was crumpled against the wall, his eyes rolling back and the print from Adriano's fist livid on his jaw.

He wasn't happy about losing control, but to finally pay Crane back for all his smart remarks, to finally admit that he did understand and it pissed him off—yeah, that felt good.

And it felt great to defend Lil. To claim her in front of all them.

He breathed heavily as he stared down at Crane, shaking out his aching hand. The rest of the room was silent.

And then: "Jesus, I think you broke his jaw."

Adriano didn't know who'd said it. His attention was on the sound of steps coming down the hallway, then the rodeo official appearing in the doorway, taking in the scene. The official who must have heard that last comment.

"Mr. Silva," the official said grimly, "you're going to have to come with me."

ADRIANO STAGGERED along the hotel hallway, his legs numb, his insides hollow.

His phone buzzed in his back pocket, but he ignored it. As he had for the past six—seven?—hours. He fumbled for the room card in the same pocket, the phone angrily vibrating against his hand as he did.

The door handle flashed green once he got the damn card in, and he stumbled into the room.

Darkness greeted him. She wasn't there.

He hung on to the door handle for a moment, halfway in, halfway out. He'd expected her to be there, waiting for him. But he wasn't certain he was disappointed she wasn't.

She'd slept with Crane. And what had happened after—

"Adriano?" Watery. Uncertain. From a far corner in the darkened room.

He froze. She was there. And she'd been crying.

"It's me." His voice was a deep scrape, exhaustion bleeding out of it.

She flipped on the light. Her face was blotchy, bone white beneath the patches of red staining her eyes and cheeks. She looked as if she'd been weeping for hours.

His heart twisted into a knot similar to the one his gut was already in. He shut the door softly behind him.

"Where have you been?" Fresh tears began to slide down her cheeks. "They announced that you wouldn't be riding in the rest of the event but didn't say why. And I called and called and called, but you never answered. I thought..." Her voice died as she turned her face away.

"After seeing you get hung up, I thought something terrible had happened."

Something terrible had happened. But not like she thought.

When he didn't answer, she looked up. "Why didn't you answer? What happened?" Panic made the edges of her words razor sharp.

He blinked at her. The mother of his child. The woman he'd thrown a kiss to in front of a thousand people. "Did you sleep with Crane?"

The redness drained from her face, leaving only bleached white behind. "What?"

The starkness of that almost hurt him. Almost. "Colby Crane? An asshole, about so tall? Blond, blue eyed? A bull rider?" He was hurting her, he could tell. He kept on. "The son of a bitch that I have to pretend to be an idiot with so I don't beat the shit out of him?"

She put her fingertips to her lips. "He's the one. The one who makes comments to you. And you pretend not to understand." The realization made her voice soft.

Fuck softness. He was done with that and with pretending. His rage and its expression were all too real. The consequences as well. "So you do know him." He put more than a drop of acid into his words. "Did. You. Fuck. Him?"

The color returned to her face as she lifted her chin, her eyes narrowing. "Yeah. About a year ago." Defiant. Daring him to strike back.

So he did. "You fucked that asshole? How could you?"

"What do you want me to say? He was terrible? He was great?" She spread her hands wide. "Or how about: it's none of your fucking business?"

He'd just punched the man because of it. So yes, it *was* his fucking business. "Crane made it my business by shoving that information in my face. Right before I beat the shit out of him."

She gasped. "You did what?"

"I slammed him into a wall and punched him in the jaw." It had felt great at the time—not so much now. And this next bit had felt terrible from the moment he'd heard it: "So I've been suspended from the tour for the rest of the year."

A few years more. A few dollars more. But no more money this particular year. No top-ten finish. Maybe no championship next year. And as for going home…

He blew out a hard breath, rubbed his forehead. *Fuck.* And all because he'd had to shut Crane's smart mouth.

"The rest of the year?" Lil's jaw dropped. "What did you do to him?"

"He's fine." Well, his jaw was bruised and his ribs too, most likely, but otherwise, Crane was fine. She didn't need to worry about him. "I think they wanted to make an example of me."

"Let me get this straight: Crane tells you I slept with him —and you *hit him?*" Her face was tight with anger, one hand on her belly and the other clenched into a fist.

"I did it to defend you." He'd been suspended for *her.* Didn't she understand? He'd lost all that money for *her.*

"Defend me?" She gestured sharply toward herself. "What danger was I in? I wasn't even there."

Didn't she care at all about her reputation? He certainly did. "He said he'd slept with you. In front of everyone." She was *his*—of course he was going to fight back when someone said shit like that.

She set both hands on her belly as she glared at him. "Who else are you going to punch for me?"

Realization turned the knot in his gut into a coil of ice. *It wasn't only Crane.* His throat frosted with pain, coating his words with bitterness. "Who else have you slept with?"

She shook her head, began to gather her things. "Not twice in one day. I'm not doing this twice in one day. And to think that I was going to tell you—" Her fingers curled tight around the handle of her bag.

He didn't know what she meant, but he understood that she was readying to leave. He set his back against the door. No way in hell was he letting her go. "Who was it? How many of them have been laughing behind my back?"

"It's none of your business! None of it is." She hefted her bag onto her shoulder, one hand wrapped around her bump as if protecting the baby from him. "Now let me out."

"No. You're mine. And I'm not letting you go." She didn't get to run away from this, from what she'd done to him.

"Oh no. You aren't going to do this." She stabbed her forefinger at him. "It's all about the baby, remember? No sex, remember? And now I'm yours?" She put her hand on his shoulder, tried to shove him away. "Fuck you."

His heart twisted with anger. Or pain. Or both. He'd done all this for *her.* The fear on her face after his ride, the way Crane had sneered her name, his suspension—it was all because of how he felt about her.

He loved her.

Swallowing hard as that realization pushed through his rage, he looked down at her tearstained face. Her jaw was rigid, her eyes blazing, and her hand was still trying to push him away. He caught at it. "Lil, I—"

"Don't try to explain." She snatched her hand away, her eyes going hard. "I didn't sign up for this caveman jealousy act. I should have known from the beginning when you first started to throw your weight around that we'd end up here."

Her crying. Him blocking her escape. Jesus, what was wrong with him?

He stepped away from the door. "I'm sorry."

The anger was entirely gone, only shame left. Shame that he could love her and yet treat her like this.

"Is this how you'll treat our daughter?"

With that, she won. His shoulders sagged, and he let the wall catch him, support him.

She'd been right all along—the baby did belong with her. Not with a man who'd react like this—trapping the mother of his child because she'd slept with someone before him.

"I'm sorry." She'd rejected it before, but it was all he had. He'd lost everything else. His career, the baby—her.

"Save it." Her anger remained. "Don't call me. Don't e-mail me." She jerked the door open.

"What about Gabriela?"

She froze, her throat working. "Get a lawyer. You'll be hearing from mine. The less I see you, the more I can keep it all about the baby. And that's what we both want."

It wasn't what he wanted. Not at all. But he let her go anyway.

Chapter 14

LIL'S ASS LEFT THE SEAT AS she reached for the handle above the door, the truck jerking as it hit a bad bump. Again.

They really ought to repave the road leading out to the prison. It was more pothole than asphalt at this point. But repairing a road leading to a prison in the middle of nowhere probably wasn't big on Caltrans's priorities.

The truck hit another hole and she glanced over at Luke, who was driving. "Are you aiming for them?"

Luke flicked a glance at her, his shiner gleaming blue-black behind his sunglasses. "Shut up, Lil."

Damn, the both of them were in a good mood today. Four hours of driving and this was their first attempt at conversation.

"So, how did you get that black eye?" Might as well poke at Luke a little more. Might make her feel better. Two weeks of radio silence from Adriano had left her in a hell of a mood.

"Don't worry about it." He jerked the wheel, the truck veering for the centerline, then jerked it back, dodging a crater that must have been two feet deep. "Say, whatever happened to that Brazilian who was supposed to be living with us?"

Touché. "Tell me about the black eye and I'll tell you what happened to him."

Luke stared out at the road, the muscle in his jaw tensing. "No," he said finally. "I don't want to talk about it."

It was probably about that stupid Warrior Race he was doing for charity. He'd been paired with Ana Chacon, who ran the resort at the casino and hated Luke's guts and always had. He returned the favor. But Lil couldn't quite imagine Ana giving him a black eye.

"Okay. But then you don't get to find out what happened with..." She couldn't quite bring herself to say his name. "With that Brazilian."

"Is he gone?"

Was he gone? With the baby, he'd never truly be gone. Her hand tightened on the handle above the door. Hard to heal a broken heart when she knew she'd be forced into close contact with him, over and over again.

Except, in the two weeks since their blowup, he hadn't tried to call, he hadn't e-mailed. Just like she'd asked.

She hadn't contacted the lawyer yet. She didn't even know what she would say. *I'm in love with this man, I'm having his baby, but I want no contact with him?* Her stomach rolled even though the truck was steady. God, but she'd gotten herself in quite the mess: a heartbreaking, stomach-churning, black-rain-cloud mess.

Maybe Bob was right. Maybe she had made the wrong choice, keeping this baby. Or even in going to bed with Adriano in the first place.

She stared out at the lonely, broken, desolate road. A mirror of her mood.

It would be so much better if they could make a clean

break, if she could hide from him to lick her wounds. Seeing him again—it was going to tear her apart each and every time.

"He's the father of my kid," she said finally. "He's never going to be *gone* gone."

Luke only grunted and drove them over another pothole.

Depressing didn't quite cover the jail. It was dreary, institutional, a leaden weight that settled on her skin. The grass was entirely dead, nothing but bare dirt, asphalt, and cinder block. The razor wire cutting through marked the strict boundary between what was kept inside and the open space outside.

She and Luke went through the metal detectors, got patted down, received their visitor's badges, and went in to see Josh.

The years in jail had made him slimmer, but not really thin. More like jail was carving away the unessential bits of him. He wore his thousand-yard stare, a relatively new thing for him. When he'd first come, he'd been pissed. Pissed that this had happened to him, that he'd actually been sent to jail. That he would be stuck there for years. Pissed that Benedict thought he deserved this and had told him so.

Lil had done her best to soothe him, because while he did kind of deserve it, it still sucked. Nothing had helped though, except for time. The anger had drained away over the years, leaving this grayscale copy of what had once been Josh.

"Hey." Their brother's smile was wan, the same beige as his prison-issued clothes.

"Hey." Luke waved. *No touching*—that was the first rule of prison visits.

Lil waved herself, maneuvered into the hard plastic

chair. Her normally agile body was turning into an ocean tanker—she was going to need the help of some tugboats to do tight turns by the end of this.

"Hey, Josh. You look good." He didn't—his eyes were hollow, his expression weary. She'd thought he'd perk up as the end of his sentence came near, but he only seemed to get more depressed.

"Thanks." Josh's smile didn't brighten. "You look a little bigger. How's the baby?"

"She's good. I can feel her moving now. And I'm having the big ultrasound tomorrow." She smiled wide at him, hoping he'd catch some of her joy. Not that she had a ton to spare at the moment.

"That's great." He nodded slowly, as if processing the disconnect between his words and his mood. "Nice eye there, Luke."

Luke reddened. "Yeah. Hurts like a bastard."

Lil held her breath—Josh was actually teasing Luke. Gently, but still a tease.

Before, Josh had been the biggest comic in the family. There wasn't a joke he wouldn't make, a prank he wouldn't pull. But that had all ended when he'd been sent here.

She waited for Josh to make another joke, to show another spark of the old him. But the silence stretched on.

Lil searched for more to say. "Have you seen Mom and Dad recently?"

"Yeah. Last week."

Lil knew better than to ask about Benedict. Their eldest brother had been to visit a few months ago, but neither Josh nor Benedict would discuss it. Even Pilar was uncharacteristically silent about it.

"How's Leonora?" Josh asked.

That fell like a rock into the stillness between them. Lil

couldn't ever remember Josh asking about Leonora. At least not to her.

When Josh had crashed that car, he'd almost killed Leonora. Lil had never breathed the woman's name to her brother again, although someone must have kept him updated on her condition. She flicked a glance at Luke, who was nodding. Must have been Luke then.

"She's... fine." Luke had to struggle to find that descriptor. "I saw Jackson last week and he said she was good."

Jackson was Leonora's brother and the same age as Luke. Leonora had been bubbly and fun before the accident, a perfect foil for Josh's jovial antics. But she didn't get out much these days.

"Good." Josh examined his hands, which were gripping each other tightly. "I'm glad to hear it."

The silence stretched further. What to talk about after that? Bringing up the situation with Adriano was only going to make everyone feel worse.

"I'm getting the space above the garage ready for you," Luke said. "Hope you're ready to get woken up by a baby in a few months."

"Thanks." Josh turned his blank stare toward the window. "I won't mind. Is Adriano going to be able to help at night?"

So much for avoiding the Adriano situation. Lil blew out a breath. "Yeah, he's... We kind of broke up." Not that they'd really been together. But describing the depth of her heartache in the middle of a prison visit wasn't something she was up for at the moment.

Josh's gaze swung back, took on some clarity. "You guys are having a baby together. And you broke up?"

She frowned down at the table surface, which was worn

down by however many hands had touched it over the years. "It's... it's complicated."

She wanted Adriano, she loved him... but she wouldn't be tied down by him. And certainly not for stuff she'd done before she'd even met him.

And she didn't even know what to do about the custody agreement now. The lawyers would have to hammer that out.

"Huh." Josh's tilted his head. "What happened? Last time we talked, things were going good."

Man, of all the things for Josh to show some interest in. She chewed on her lip, pondered what to say.

Luke rolled his eyes. "I already tried. She doesn't want to talk about it."

"Oh? Let's talk about that eye of yours then," she countered.

Josh laughed. A small laugh, but a laugh. She and Luke shared a quick smile. They could still make their brother laugh.

"Okay, we won't talk about it." Josh's smile faded. "But he's been to your doctor's appointments so far. Is he going to the ultrasound tomorrow?"

"I'm not sure if I want him there." She certainly hadn't intended to call and remind Adriano. First, she'd been angry, then she'd been sad, and now? "I mean, I can send the pictures after." It sounded lame, keeping him away from that appointment, when it had made so much sense in her head before.

Josh's expression went distant again. "Whatever makes you happiest."

Great. Even her brother in prison thought she was doing this wrong.

And it didn't make her happy. Not at all. She missed

Adriano, didn't even know where he was, what he was going to do now that he was suspended... She worried about him.

"I suppose I should tell him." She wriggled her toes in her boots to ease her guilt. "If he wants to get here on time."

"Yeah." An amused spark lit Josh's eyes. "Might want to get on that."

"You can have your big make-up phone call on the way home," Luke said. "That'll be fun to listen in on."

At that, the light in Josh's eyes dimmed. "You guys better get going. Thanks for coming."

He was right—but after the glimmers of the old Josh she'd seen today, it especially hurt to leave him here. Even though he'd be home in a few months. They said good-bye and left him in that place, looking hollow eyed once more.

She and Luke walked back to the truck in silence, their earlier mood returning. Flatter now though—a prison visit always did that, left her feeling run over by a steamroller.

As they drove away, she stared at her phone, waiting for a signal. Hoping that the phone wouldn't grab one too soon, would give her a little more time to collect herself. To prepare to hear his voice again.

One bar. Two. And then five. She sighed. No more excuses.

"Do you know Colby Crane?" she asked.

This wasn't a stalling tactic on her part—she just wanted to think out the situation more before she talked to Adriano.

"Huh?" Luke adjusted his eyeglasses, wincing when he brushed his bruised eye. "Yeah, I've met him a couple of times. Heard stories from John and Shorty. Why?"

Either Luke was pretty shocked to have her bring up Colby right now... or he didn't like the guy.

She picked at her thumbnail. "I slept with him last year."

She ignored Luke's groan of disgust. "Adriano found out, beat up Crane, and we fought. That's why it's over."

"Crane's a fucking asshole. Why would you sleep with him?"

"I only did it the once! Don't tell me you've never regretted something the next morning?"

He unconsciously touched a finger to under his bruised eye. "Not as much as I regret knowing that my sister slept with Crane. Look, the man's a shit stirrer. I'm not saying beating him up was right—or fighting with you about it was either—but Crane's pissed off a lot of people. He might have had it coming."

"Violence is always wrong," she said. "Although Adriano did tell me that Crane liked to poke at him. Make smart comments and stuff." Not that it excused what he'd done—especially Adriano's comments to her after—but she wasn't known to have the calmest temper herself.

"Huh. And you guys haven't tried to discuss this rationally, have you?"

Nope. She'd told him to stay away. And he had.

"Why are you defending him all of a sudden?" Not accusing, just curious.

Luke shrugged. "He seemed to make you happy. Look, if he's a jealous punk, I'll be the first to say stay away. But maybe you should try talking it over with him."

"Maybe." She turned the phone over in her hands, watched the light slide across the brushed metal. They did need to talk about it. But first, she had to invite him to the ultrasound. "Want to talk about your eye now?"

"Nope."

She sighed, then called up Adriano, her heart hammering in her ears. What if he didn't pick up? Or worse, what if he did?

"Hello?" So deep. It was like biting into a square of the darkest chocolate, hearing his voice. Sweet and bitter and rich all at once.

"Hey." She sounded like a chicken being strangled. She cleared her throat. "Um, it's Lil."

"I know." Oh so carefully neutral. He wasn't giving her anything here.

"There's uh…" She rubbed at her forehead, hyperaware of Luke listening in. "Do you remember that the big ultrasound is tomorrow?"

"Yes." Still flat. Still giving nothing away.

If he'd missed her, he certainly wasn't showing it. A lump collected in her throat. "Did you still want to come? I mean, if you're anywhere close—"

"I'm in California."

He was? "Oh."

"I wanted to be near you in case you needed something. You or the baby."

Oh, God. He'd been there, close to her, quiet because she'd asked him. But ready if she needed him.

Yeah, they did need to talk.

She blinked hard, pulling in a shaky breath. "Okay, so you can make it." The lump traveled to her chest, made her lungs tight. "Eleven. Do you remember how to get to the doctor's? I'll meet you there."

"Yes." Something vibrated deep beneath that. Pain? Anguish?

No, no, no. She had her own pain to work through—she couldn't take on his. "Okay. See you then." And she disconnected before she could fall apart completely.

ADRIANO WATCHED as the nurse took the blood pressure cuff off Lil's arm, examined it, then put it back on.

The nurse was the only one wearing any kind of expression—he and Lil sat in stony silence. She hadn't even looked at him when he'd arrived at the doctor's office, so he'd taken the hint and kept his mouth shut as he sat down next to her.

The machine whirred as the cuff filled with air. Lil winced when it fully inflated. He suppressed his own twinge of sympathy. She wanted to think him a monster? Then he'd play the monster for her. Whatever she wanted, he'd give her.

Including their child.

The nurse frowned at the numbers like she had at the first set.

Lil stared straight ahead, back rigid, mouth flat.

"Is something the matter?" he asked the nurse. Lil might not care that something could be wrong, but he did.

The nurse pinched up her mouth apologetically. "You'll have to speak with the doctor and see what she says."

As if that was reassuring. At least the nurse wasn't calling the doctor in right away, so it couldn't be life threatening.

Lil gave no indication she'd heard any of it. She moved like a zombie toward the ultrasound room, lay down on the table with all the liveliness of a robot.

After two weeks of silence from her—silence that had killed him to carry on, silence that he'd honored at her request—he'd hoped her invitation might be an opportunity to fix what he'd broken. To repair their relationship. But it was clear this was an obligation to her and nothing more. He was there because it was right for the father of the baby to be present. Not because Lil actually wanted him.

He settled into the chair and waited for another glimpse of his daughter. That would be the only joy from this visit.

This time he recognized more of his baby. Her face, her hands, her feet, all of her wriggling constantly. Did Lil feel that, all that motion inside her? He didn't know and was afraid to ask in case Lil refused to answer.

Lil kept her gaze hard on the ultrasound screen, never letting him glimpse even a hint of her reaction.

For him, the experience was as wondrous as the first time. He'd only seen Gabriela twice now, but he already knew he'd never tire of looking at her. And that the time he spent apart from her, the long months she'd spend with Lil, would hurt with a depth he'd never experienced before.

"Everything looks good," the tech said, "but the doctor will be in to talk to you as well. Are you ready to see the sex?"

Lil nodded.

"Okay." The tech prodded with the wand and peered at the screen. Adriano had at least had some idea of what he was looking at before—he had no clue what was happening here.

"It's a girl!" the tech announced. "Congratulations. Have you thought about names?"

They had a name. One they'd chosen together at that baby store, where they'd picked out all the things they'd thought the baby would need.

Adriano waited for Lil to say it. She was the mother— she had first rights.

But when she kept silent, he said, "Gabriela." At the exact same time Lil did.

Their gazes met for the first time that day, and that old spark passed between them, the one that kicked his heart into high gear.

"What a beautiful name." The tech probably said that to every couple who came through, but she sounded like she really meant it this time.

"Thank you," Lil said, never looking away from him.

He held her gaze. *I love you. I love this baby. And I'm sorry.* All the things he wanted to say but couldn't. Not with the tech watching.

Lil's expression was clear, her gaze steady. Did she see in his eyes how he felt? Did she care?

The doctor came in then, severing the moment between them. "And how are the two of you?"

Lil tore her gaze from his. "I'm fine."

The doctor glanced up at her tone, looked between the two of them. "Really? Because your blood pressure is elevated." Dr. Young set a hand to her chin, studying the both of them as the tech slipped out behind her. "Is anything happening that's causing you stress?"

He slid a glance to Lil. Now how was she going to answer that?

"I..." Lil closed her mouth, folded her hands together.

This was his fault. He ought to take the blame. "It was me. I—"

"We're rethinking living together." Lil lifted her chin, set her jaw. Was that dare in her eyes for the doctor? Or for him?

He raised an eyebrow at her. She didn't need to do that. He'd already been halfway to admitting that *he'd* fucked everything up.

"I see." Dr. Young's fingers tapped against her chin. "Well, that complicates things. Because based on your blood pressure reading, I'm going to recommend at least a week of bed rest."

"What!" Lil shook her head wildly. "I can't lie around for a whole week. I have work to do."

His own blood pressure skyrocketed. "Is she all right?" he demanded. "Should she be admitted to the hospital?"

Lil turned her glare on him, but he didn't back down. Her health was important. And she was everything to him.

"No, no," the doctor said. "It's a little high—something we want to keep an eye on, but nothing serious. Yet."

That slowed Lil down, her throat working as she swallowed. "If it's not serious, why do I need to be on bed rest?"

Adriano tightened his jaw, the pressure making his ears ache. If she wasn't going to take the doctor's warnings seriously...

Her tearstained face. His body, blocking her escape.

There was nothing he could do. Not against her will.

"Well, if your blood pressure doesn't come down," Dr. Young said, "you could be on bed rest for the rest of the pregnancy. So a week, just to be careful, really isn't much. Is there anyone who can take care of you?" Her gaze swung to Adriano.

Well, he *had* found himself with some free time on his hands. Too bad Lil didn't want him anywhere near her.

The corners of Lil's eyes crinkled, worry finally stealing across her face. "Bea's going away on some camping trip, and Luke has to work during the day." She tugged at her fingers. "I guess I could call my mom."

Not once did she look at him.

Fuck it. "I'll do it."

She was the mother of his child—she might not want him there, but he owed her this at least. He wouldn't touch her, would only talk to her when necessary—it would be purely minimal contact. Just as she wanted.

He might have imagined it, but there was a spark of approval in the doctor's eyes.

Lil didn't look approving—she looked apprehensive. But at least she was meeting his gaze now. "Are you sure?" An edge there, as if she suspected him of something.

But she hadn't said no.

"I've got nowhere to be," he pointed out gently. No pushing. Letting her come to him. But his pulse surged as he willed her to say yes.

She licked her lips, studied him with a keen expression.

Come on, Lil. Let me help you. Let me make this up to you.

She swallowed, looked to her lap. "Okay." Muted, without a hint of a dare or defiance.

He released a breath. "Okay. Good." His heart quieted. He wasn't going to fuck this up. Not this time.

"Good." Dr. Young snapped closed Lil's chart. "One week of nothing but sitting on the couch. You can sit up, go to the bathroom, shower—just take it easy. Rest. Let Adriano take care of you. Think you can handle it?"

The doctor's gaze flicked to him, then back to Lil. The doctor was definitely up to something, but he couldn't quite figure what.

Lil gave a sad little nod. But she'd agreed.

Afterward, they walked out to her truck together, neither one speaking. The awkwardness between them was like a giant balloon, one that Adriano bounced against whenever he got too close to her.

He opened the truck door for her, held out his hand to help her in.

She stared at it for a moment.

"I'm very sorry," he said quietly. "I never should have behaved like that." He didn't usually behave like that—the one time he finally lost his temper, and he lost Lil as well.

"It... I'm not going to say it was okay. Because it wasn't. But thank you." Her gaze met his, steady, questioning. "How long has Colby been fucking with you?"

He frowned as he thought back. "Years, I guess. Since I first met him."

She fiddled with her purse strap, then took on a stern expression. "It was still wrong to hit him."

"Yes. And I've been punished," he reminded her. Losing his place on the tour, losing her... He'd return to the tour next year, but he found he didn't care as much about bull riding anymore.

As for the money, there was enough to support his mother, his daughter, and his family. Not as much as he might have liked, but enough to go home now.

Everything he'd feared was happening—losing his place on the circuit, falling short of the plan he'd set, leaving part of his heart and his child behind here—but strangely the fear was muted.

There was only determination that he should make this up to her.

Her mouth pinched, as if she was struggling to hold on to her anger. "You shouldn't have been such a dick about who I've slept with. It really is none of your business."

"I know." He tilted his head, studied her eyes. Was she forgiving him? "Don't worry, my mother scolded me for a long while. She told me I had been raised better than that. And she was right."

"Your mother?" Her eyes went wide with surprise, more green than gray in the bright light. "You told your mother?"

"Yes. I like to tell her when I've made terrible mistakes so she can tell me how to fix them." He gave her a small, wry smile.

His mother had told him to stay in America until he fixed things with Lil. He knew better than to disobey her.

Lil didn't return his smile. "What if I told you I've slept with every single bull rider on the tour?" A dare. Always the challenges with this nervy woman.

And he loved her for it.

He tried a joke. "I'd admire your stamina."

Her lips twitched.

"Don't laugh," he said. "It only encourages me."

She shook her head as the smile broke out across her face. Not quite forgiveness, not quite setting them back to where they'd been—but a start.

He'd take it.

She set her hand in his, and he lifted her into the truck. She leaned out. "I'll see you at home then?"

He nodded. "Sounds good to me." And it did.

Chapter 15

LIL FLIPPED THROUGH THE CHANNELS for the fourth time that morning. Six hundred channels and not a thing to watch. Bed rest was hell, and this was only the first day. Rufio was next to her, watching the TV with his head on his paws and looking as bored as she felt.

Where was Adriano? She was about to crawl out of her skin, wondering what was going on at the bull barn. Beau said he could handle it all, and he could, but she still wanted to know.

Her e-mails too—James, her dad's friend, had said that they would look at the videos she'd sent once more. Not a definite yes, but better than the flat no they'd given before. Maybe they'd reconsidered by now and had e-mailed her to tell her. She jiggled her leg, which made Rufio lift his head eagerly.

"Sorry. We're not going anywhere."

He dropped his head and she forced her leg to be still.

A week of this. If she was supposed to be keeping calm, it would have been better to just let her keep going to work.

Her phone rang and she eagerly snatched it up. A call. An actual live human who wanted to talk to her.

"Hello?" As eager as a puppy.

"Hey." Bea sounded a little taken aback by Lil's enthusiasm. "How are you? How was the doctor's appointment?"

Great. Terrible. "We got to see the baby, which was nice. And it's definitely a girl." That had been great. Better than great. She only wished the atmosphere between her and Adriano hadn't been so oppressive. "But my blood pressure was a little high, so I'm on bed rest for a week." Which was terrible.

At least the sitting on the couch part. The having Adriano take care of her part... Well, it wasn't quite as weird as she'd expected. When she'd agreed to this, it hadn't been her good sense that had said okay. It had been her heart. She only hoped her heart hadn't made a terrible mistake. At least, not worse than falling in love with him in the first place.

And his apology after the doctor's appointment... So simple. But so powerful.

And funny. She still couldn't quite believe he'd told his mom. A dude with a history of being a jealous asshole usually didn't tell his mom he'd been a jealous asshole, did he?

So maybe it was a one-off thing. He'd certainly sounded remorseful.

Maybe they could forge a decent co-parenting relationship—this week would be a good test of that. But Lil didn't think she was ready to risk her heart again. Not when he was certain to leave her. And not when he certainly gave no hint he wanted to risk his.

And the custody thing... She was trying very hard not to think of that. That was certain to raise her blood pressure.

She'd woken up this morning at her usual time, but Adriano had already been awake, telling her he would take care of the goats and the chickens.

"I've milked goats and collected eggs," he'd reminded her as he settled her on the couch. She'd been ready to protest, but he'd placed a mug of coffee in her hands.

"I'm not certain if I should have this." But Lord, did she want it.

"You're going to be sitting on this couch for a week, which will be torture for you. A cup of coffee won't hurt." He gestured to the home blood pressure monitor he'd picked up yesterday. "Take a reading this morning, please."

An order, although politely couched. He'd also given her some coffee. And he was close to her, close enough to almost touch...

She leaned back, put the mug to her lips just to busy herself as she listened to him leave. Her blood pressure was normal according to the machine, but she kept her butt on the couch. She'd be a good little patient this week so there'd be no excuse to keep her there another week.

He'd come back from taking care of her stock and made her breakfast. As she'd eaten under his watchful eye, his attention making her heart do jumpy things, he'd asked, "What needs to be done with the bulls?"

She paused. Beau would be there, and he could handle things without her this week—but there was some stuff she wanted to tell him. And Adriano would be the perfect messenger. Maybe she could keep him shuttling between here and the barns, carrying instructions for her. Not as good as being there herself, but better than nothing. And he wouldn't be so temptingly near all the time.

"Could you go talk to Beau?" she asked.

He'd nodded, then listened patiently to all her instructions for the bull barns. After her third reminder about a delivery that was supposed to come, he'd held up a hand and asked, "Do you want your laptop?"

Her laptop would be awesome. But would working on it violate the bed rest decree? "Can I have it?"

"I don't see why not, as long as you stay on the couch. And you can send more instructions to Beau and me by e-mail." He'd given a brief smile. "That should be fun for you."

Her heart had twisted at his smile. And at his general attitude. He wasn't commanding her, he wasn't throwing his weight around—he was trying to make this as pleasant as possible for her.

This was the Adriano she loved. Bittersweet to get that Adriano this last week together.

"Bed rest?" Bea's voice snapped her thoughts back to their conversation. "Who's taking care of you?"

"It's only for a week, just as a precaution." Which didn't really answer Bea's question. "Adriano is here."

"*Ooooh.*" Bea knew the whole sordid tale. "Are you okay with that? I can cancel my trip."

"Things are... fine." Except for how sad Adriano looked. And how quiet he was. And how she wanted to touch him but didn't dare. "He's bringing me my laptop."

"Wow. That's better than roses." For once Bea didn't sound as if she were dryly tweaking her cousin. Bea probably did think a laptop was better than roses.

"Don't cancel your trip for me." Although it was sweet of Bea. "What are you going there to get again?"

"I finally got a permit to harvest some nightshade penstemon. It only grows on the east side of the San Jacintos at a very specific elevation."

"The government gave you permission to kill an endangered plant?"

"Not all of it. And it's for science."

Lil smiled at Bea's exasperated tone. She was so easy to rile. "Who's this dude Luke found to guide you?"

"Uh, some firefighter he's friends with." Bea sounded more interested in the plants than the man. "Russell Cheng."

"Oh, I know him. Nice guy. Kind of goofy."

She could almost hear the needle scratch in Bea's brain. "Goofy? What do you mean by goofy?" Bea didn't do goofy. Or silly. Or even fun, really. She'd brought home some sullen assholes at times.

"I mean he looks exactly like Goofy. Even played him at Disneyland one summer." She bit her lip to keep from laughing.

"Very funny, Liliana." Back to the exasperated tone. "Speaking of goofy."

"No, he really is nice," Lil assured her. "He'll take good care of you. He leads backpacking trips every weekend out there."

The back door opened, sending Rufio scrambling over the back of the couch to bark at whoever was there.

Adriano, with her laptop. Her skin pulled tight with electric awareness. But she was excited to get some work done, not to see him.

"That's Adriano now," she told Bea. "Have fun on your camping trip. Don't get lost in the woods or kidnapped by hippies."

"It's a wilderness area. No one's going to be there. Except for me and Fireman Goofy."

Lil laughed. "Love you, coz. Take care."

"Love you too. Take care of yourself. And of that baby."

Lil ended the call and stared at the phone wistfully for a moment. Bea really was an awesome cousin. She hoped this backpacking trip wasn't too much for Bea's carefully culti-vated type A personality.

Adriano came in, her precious laptop cradled in his hands. Such long, strong fingers.

Stop that.

He handed it over. "No getting off the couch, remember." More orders. She'd actually kind of missed it. "I'll talk to Beau and be back in an hour."

"You can stay longer if you want." She carefully studied his reaction, even as she kept her tone casual. "To help Beau." He wouldn't want to sit around on the couch with her all day. He wasn't built for that any more than she was.

His eyes went dark. "I'm here to help you."

A shiver ran across her skin at the low, rough words. Almost as if he was saying much, much more than that.

But he was back out the door before she could puzzle it out.

A WEEK LATER, Lil was on the phone with Dr. Young. "My blood pressure looks great. And it has all week. Can I get off bed rest now?" She sounded like a kid begging for a Popsi-cle, but she was so, so sick of the couch.

And being in such close quarters with Adriano... Torment. Purest torment. She had to get away from him before her heart cracked any further.

"Hmm. It could stand to go a bit lower," Dr. Young said.

Lower? Any lower and Lil would be dead. "Uhh…"

"Can Adriano stay on a little longer to care for you?

Another week of bed rest wouldn't hurt. Remember, we want what's best for the baby."

How was she supposed to argue with that? "Let me ask him."

She moved the phone away from her mouth, her heart beginning to pound. He was right next to her on the couch, listening to her side of the conversation attentively. "Can you stay longer? I know you wanted to get back home."

She kept her voice casual, just a friend asking another friend for a favor. They'd been *friends* this week, friends without benefits, even though it was miserable. At least for her.

He'd seemed perfectly content with it. And he actually hadn't said he wanted to go back to Mato Grosso do Sul right away, but where else would he go until next year's tour? Of course he wanted to return home. He talked to his mom at least twice a day, and she was sick, and... and he'd always been firm on that. He was leaving here someday. Someday soon.

Her heart sounded loud in her ears as she waited for his reply, her mouth going dry.

"I can stay." He didn't sound regretful or annoyed—only steady. He might agree to anything she asked of him with that even tone, happy to do whatever she requested.

She let out a shaky breath. She shouldn't want him to stay so badly, not when she knew he wanted to leave, not when it meant more bed rest for her—but she still did all the same. "He can stay," she told the doctor, relief putting a wobble in her voice.

"Great!" Wow, Dr. Young sounded really happy about it. "I'll talk to you in a week then. Keep resting!"

Lil put down the phone. Another week. Another week on the couch, of being *just friends* with the man she loved...

She blew out a breath. This was how it would be when the baby came. She should get used to it now.

And she still hadn't called the lawyer.

"Thanks," she said weakly, staring at her phone.

"No problem." As if she'd asked him to pick something up at the store for her or an equally bland chore. "If the doctor says you need the rest..." Worry shaded his tone there. "Then it really is best for the baby."

Best for the baby of course. But not her heart.

A WEEK AFTER THAT, Lil was canning peaches. Her early trees were finishing up and the late ones were starting, so they were awash in peaches. Adriano ate one at least every hour—she ate two, one for her and one for the baby—but even with that and grilled peaches and peach pie, they still had too many.

She and Adriano had agreed in the middle of the second week, with her blood pressure holding steady at a pretty low reading, that bed rest could be interpreted more as house rest. She hadn't fought for more; he hadn't fought to keep her on the couch. An easy agreement, which made it all the more painful.

She didn't leave the house. Adriano did all the chores—taking care of the goats and the chickens and the garden and the orchard—and also went down to the bull barns for a few hours each day to help Beau and report back to her.

They didn't share a bed—he'd made no move to touch her unnecessarily, not even once—but they shared everything else. They'd fallen into an idyll of domesticity, living in quiet contentment. It was nice... but she missed their fire. Of course, fire got a person burned.

And it would end, no matter how nice it was.

And she still hadn't called the lawyer.

She sighed as she set the lid on the pot. No sense wishing for more heartache. Their present situation held more than enough for her.

He watched her closely as she put the lid on, no doubt in case he had to save her from the stove at some point. But he was smiling. "When do they pop?" he asked.

"Once they're cooling on the counter. You've got to be patient." She set the oven timer. "Come December, when we're only dreaming of fresh peaches, we can have these."

His smile dimmed.

Damn. He wouldn't be here in December. Which raised the sticky question of how they were going to split holidays. She pushed that away. She was supposed to be stress free right now.

"I'm going to check my e-mail," she told him. "You can stay here and wait for the timer if you want."

He shook his head and followed her into the living room. He settled next to her on the couch, then laid his arm behind her.

She froze in the middle of entering her password. He hadn't touched her once. Hadn't even made her think he wanted to touch her.

It had hurt along with everything else, knowing that his attraction to her was gone. Only, maybe it wasn't. He didn't usually sit like that on the couch. And he was closer to her than he'd been... in forever.

Don't think about it. Don't expect anything. It will only hurt worse if you expect things.

She finished entering her password. And opened the first message with dread.

Bob Stanton. If he wanted to scold her again...

Only he didn't.

She leaned toward Adriano, tapped him on the belly. God, it was firm. "Look at this. Bob changed his mind. He thought about what I said, and he's decided to sell me those cows." She smiled at the laptop. Huh. Apparently it had been a good idea to be conciliatory with him. Not that she still wasn't pissed about what Bob had said—but at least she was getting her cows from him.

Finally, a victory. A small one, but she'd take it. Maybe a bigger one was on the way. She still hadn't heard back from the rodeo committee.

"That's great. Compromise works, huh?" His arm slipped down the back of the couch a hair. But didn't land on her.

She scrolled through the rest of her messages, aware of how close he was. Aware of how he wasn't touching her. She ached with it, her skin crackling with the urge to touch him, if only accidentally.

Why didn't he do something? Did he even know he was tormenting her?

She decided to be daring. She used to be daring with him, before she'd lost her heart to him.

She scooted down, set her head on his thigh, resettled her laptop onto her belly. It made a good table now.

She peeped up at him. His lips were slightly parted, his gaze hooded. "Do you want to watch some videos with me?" As if she lay like this every day with him. "The Birmington ranch just put a bunch of their latest bulls out."

"Sure." But it felt like he was agreeing to something else. Something more intimate, judging by the darkening of his eyes.

She called up the videos, started the first one. Halfway through the second video, he set his hand on her hair. Not on her scalp, only on her hair. Then he began to stroke the strands as they lay across his thigh. Gentle, soothing strokes that lulled her into a half-asleep state. The video played on, but neither of them was watching.

She watched him through half-closed eyes as he kept on with his gentle caresses. His breathing was slow and deep, as if he were as hypnotized by this as she was.

Then *ding, ding, ding* from the kitchen.

She smiled up at him, feeling sleepily content. "They're done."

He didn't answer. Instead, he lowered his head and kissed her, soft and slow. Like they'd never really kissed before. No heat, although it was warm, no passion, although it was intimate. It wasn't a kiss that would lead them to sweaty wrestling on the couch—the kiss itself was both the journey and the destination.

It was delicious and agonizing all at once. Delicious because he was touching her again after all this time. Agonizing because she loved him and this kiss felt like... like *love*. And for all his care and concern the past few weeks, she wasn't certain that he loved her. Not like she did him.

After several long moments, he lifted his head. His gaze was intent, heavy, emotion pooled in his golden eyes. He wanted to tell her something.

She waited, breath still. *Maybe...*

But he only said, "Let's check the peaches. I want to hear the pop."

She let him help her off the couch, pushed her disappointment away, held the tears deep in her throat. *Don't expect anything.*

It was good that she didn't—or at least tried not to—because he didn't touch her again.

THREE WEEKS in and her blood pressure was still fine. And Dr. Young said she still needed to be on modified bed rest. But they'd "discuss" it at tomorrow's appointment.

Lil didn't even know what was going on anymore with the doctor—was her blood pressure something to worry about or not? And she certainly didn't know what was going on with Adriano.

At the moment, they were cleaning up after dinner, working together in quiet harmony. Luke was gone again— he was up to something, but she wasn't sure what—so it was only her and Adriano. As it had been for the past three weeks.

But tomorrow, if the doctor lifted her bed rest, Adriano could be gone. Would be gone. He'd said nothing about staying. It hurt to think of him gone, the two of them only meeting to hand off Gabriela, but it was more than time to pull this Band-Aid off.

She set the last plate in the dishwasher and cheerily said, "If Dr. Young says I can come off bed rest tomorrow, you can head back home. Visit your mom, see how she's doing." She said it like it was the best thing in the world— for both of them. "I know you miss it. And her."

Surprising that even though all of her ached to say that, she managed to keep the pain out of her voice.

He placed a pan in the drying rack with deliberation, his expression shuttered. "I do miss Brazil. It will be nice to visit." *Visit*. That was an interesting choice. "I haven't been back in years, you know."

She swallowed hard as she shut the dishwasher. She hadn't known that. She wasn't planning on asking him to stay, but after hearing that, she knew she absolutely couldn't.

But she'd known that all along, hadn't she?

"Well, now you can have a nice long visit. Until the tour starts up again. Or I guess until the baby's born." Her voice caught on that, on the agony of having to see him again, but not being with him. She curled her fingers around the counter, held on for dear life. It was that or grab for him one last time.

"Lil." A rough, needy scrape as he pulled her hands from the counter. And then he was kissing her, all raw want and bitter desire.

She kissed him back just the same, fire igniting along her veins. If this was how they'd say good-bye, she'd take it. After all, this was how they'd said hello, way back in Vegas.

He'd be leaving soon. Perhaps not tomorrow, but he would, in the end. Taking her heart, and perhaps even their baby.

She anchored his face between her hands, devoured his mouth, because if this was the last scrap of him she could have, she'd snatch as much as she could.

He unbuttoned his jeans with sharp, urgent movements, never giving up her mouth. He spun her around, pressed her against the counter, careful of her belly. A quick flip of her skirt, a tug at her panties, still not fast enough—it would never be fast enough for her—and then he was inside her.

The counter was cold and smooth beneath her palms, her neck twisted so that she might see him, and his cock was hard and urgent as he thrust inside.

This was how she loved it between them—fast, fierce, the pleasure building to a razor-sharp peak in seconds.

His mouth rubbed along her neck, stubble scraping, lips caressing, and soft phrases of Portuguese pouring into her ears. He was pleading with her, begging for something, but she didn't know those words—he hadn't taught them to her. So she couldn't answer.

Instead, she pressed back against him, asking for more, telling him he could take what he needed. And, in the process, give her what she needed.

She heard the smack of his hand coming against the counter, his taut arm pressing hard against her side as he braced himself. His free hand slipped around, found her clit and teased it. Oh Jesus. In this position, with him still muttering against her neck—she was going to come hard and soon.

He shifted his stance, hoisted her onto his thighs, her heels leaving the floor as his fingers kept working her clit, his cock moving deep within her. A few thrusts like that, held so precariously but so tightly by him, and she was done. The climax was sharp and sustained, almost painful in its shattering.

And it would be the last time.

One last thrust, a final plea that she still couldn't understand, and he came inside her, warmth and wetness beginning to slide down her thigh.

The tears slipped from her eyes then to fall to the counter beneath her face. Adriano breathed hard on her neck as he set her carefully back down, his cock leaving her as he did.

The tears came harder until she was fighting for air.

He turned her around and held her as she sobbed, his hand rubbing slow circles on her back. And she wept and wept, this farewell breaking her open, her grief spilling out.

This wasn't good-bye to him. She'd see him again.

This was good-bye to *them*.

Chapter 16

THEY SAT IN THE TRUCK in the parking lot of the doctor's office, neither speaking.

Adriano curled his hands around the steering wheel but didn't start the engine. He knew he needed to, but once he did, he'd start the journey home. The journey away from her.

She was gorgeous today, not that she ever wasn't, her eyes bright, her skin glowing, her body rounded with pregnancy.

As he'd held her last night while she sobbed as if her heart was breaking, he'd hoped. As he led her back to her room to tuck her into bed to sleep off her tears alone, he began to plan.

The past three weeks of not touching her, of living with her as a kind of glorified roommate, had been painful. But they'd needed it, to prove that they could get along without giving in to the fire between them.

They could work things out for their daughter. It was possible for them to be parents and nothing more.

But it would be damn painful. And empty. He knew that

now—and after Lil's tears last night, he suspected she felt the same.

Last night… when he'd imagined going back to Brazil, leaving her here alone, he couldn't hold back any longer. He'd begged her to tell him she felt the same, that she loved him as madly as he did her.

But he couldn't say it in English—it would only come in Portuguese in the moment. She had no idea what he'd asked and after when she was weeping as if her heart would break… he was too afraid. He could climb onto a bull, over and over again, but he couldn't tell her how he felt. Because she might not feel the same.

Now that the doctor had lifted the bed rest, Lil could return to her life. She didn't need him anymore. He needed her though. And he had one last bargain for her, one last way to keep her by his side. Or him by hers. Either way.

"Looks like everything's fine," she said as she stared out the windshield. Full of bright cheer and forced happiness.

Adriano suspected the doctor had other reasons for keeping Lil on bed rest so long, reasons that didn't involve her blood pressure. But he hadn't said anything, not when it fell in so well with his plans. He only had to play this last hand, *win* this last hand, and the final piece would fall into place.

"You can head out now if you want," she went on. "No need to nurse me anymore."

Her voice was all sunshine, but she was gripping the shoulder belt. Very tightly. She was a hell of a liar when she wanted to be.

"I suppose so." He kept his expression blank so as not to spook her away. To let her creep toward her feelings for him on her own time.

Come on, Lil. Come back to me.

"I mean, you can go back to Brazil. Isn't that what you always wanted?"

He savored the uncertainty in her tone. That was what he'd been waiting for. It was time to reveal all, to lay out his hand and see if she called him on it.

"I *do* want to go back. I've always wanted to go back." He turned to her then, let the intensity of his feelings shine in his eyes. "But now I want to go back with *you*."

There it was. But would she want to go back with him? She'd said once that their family ties held them tight—too tight for her to choose him?

She drew in a sharp breath. "I can't just move. My family, my work; it's all here."

Her legacy. The one she had to pass on to their daughter. His heart sank. That same old story. After these weeks together, she was circling back to where they'd started.

He had to turn her back. One last time. If this didn't work, he'd let her be. No matter how badly it would hurt.

"I can't just move either," he reminded her. "I've got more bull riding to do here, remember? At least once my suspension is over."

And his mother had told him to stay until he won Lil back. Couldn't disappoint her, now could he?

Tell her. Just tell her. But he held back, not certain why. Perhaps because this was the biggest gamble he'd ever taken, more risky than climbing onto any bull.

Lil held his heart and would hold it for the rest of her life. Not just eight seconds of it. Her and their daughter.

He couldn't go home without them.

"Then what?" she asked. "Because I know you're not offering to stay. You can't."

She wanted more from him, he could tell by the push in

her tone. She didn't want to be back where they'd started either.

He'd show her where they could go instead. Together. "How would you like to own a ranch in Mato Grosso do Sul?"

Her eyes widened with interest. "Brazil?" But she didn't make it sound impossible.

"We breed bulls here and there. And help train riders there." He was talking a little too fast, his accent thickening, but he'd gone over the details so many times—finally he could share them all with her. "Split our time between both countries. And let our daughter know both places, with both of us beside her. To inherit both her legacies."

He caught his breath, waited for her to jump in. It had come to him during their weeks together, as he'd discovered that he liked running a ranch and breeding bulls. Realized that there was a way to build a life together that could be split between their two homelands.

"Oh." Her gaze turned inward, and he could see her weighing the idea, turning it over in her head, exploring the edges of it.

He smiled wryly. "A compromise. Which is what we should have been working on all along."

Perhaps, once they'd worked the kinks out of that, they could have more.

She chewed her lip, her eyes narrow. She was going to dare him, to challenge him, he already knew. "We agreed before, no sex. To keep it focused on the baby." Her gaze was sharp now.

"And we blew that up." They couldn't help but blow that up. He was counting on them doing it again.

"What are you proposing this time?"

Proposing. He felt the same calm come over him that did

when he climbed onto the back of a bull. He took his heart into his hands, trusted that it would be safe in hers.

"Not a bargain like before," he said. "Not both of us pitted against each other and how we feel." He took a quick breath, the same kind he pulled when he nodded to the gate man to swing open the chute and start the ride. "Besides, I don't think I can agree to not sleep with the woman I love."

With those words, gave himself right to her.

Her eyes opened wide, her expression softening, a sharp, small inhale parting her lips.

He set a hand at her cheek, savoring the warmth of her, and went on. "To not touch her, to not show her all the ways I love her with my hands, my lips—"

She put her hand over his mouth. "You—why didn't you tell me sooner? I've been in agony here, being in love with you and thinking you didn't love me!"

He laughed against her hand. Only Lil would get pissed when he finally told her he loved her. And when she finally told him she loved him.

She loved him. He laughed harder, his heart bobbing in his chest. *It had all worked out.*

He wrapped his fingers around her wrist and brought her knuckles to his lips, kissing each in turn. Someday one of those fingers would wear his ring. He'd make certain of it.

But just in case—"It was wrong of me, to react that way about Crane. And to suggest this bargain with you."

She dropped her head, her gaze flitting away. "Yeah. I... I was going to tell you that night, about the baby—"

He put a finger to her lips. "I was going to tell *you* that night—you're right. The baby should be with you."

"And I was going to tell you the baby should be with *you.*"

They smiled at each other, her expression as rueful as he

felt. "I guess we've both proven that neither of us won this bargain," he said.

"Nope." She grinned now. "Which means that the baby should be with both of us. All the time. Only way to make it fair."

His heart slowed, the pump of it going deeper, more powerful. "Will you do it then? Make a life here with me? And in Brazil too? Not just for the baby, but because I love you?"

She had to say yes; he knew she would say yes—and yet he still held his breath.

"Are you trying to tie me down, Adriano Silva?"

He laughed. Forever and always a dare from her. "Can I tie you down?"

She gave a slow smile. "Maybe. Or tie me up. Or a few other things I can think of." She pulled him to her for a kiss. "Here. And in Brazil." Her lips met his, audacious as always. "Just not in front of the baby."

Epilogue

LILIANA STARED DOWN AT THE strange, tiny creature in her arms, bafflement and wonder beating through her chest. How was such a thing as this even possible?

"God, she's beautiful," she breathed. "You're beautiful," she told her daughter, her words solemn and true.

Gabriela's head was flattened, her face was scrunched, her eyes some muddy gray Lil had never seen before, and when she uncurled her fingers and toes, they were unnaturally long.

Somehow it all came together into the most wondrous thing she'd ever seen.

She'd helped make this thing. She felt as if her brain would no longer fit into her skull with that realization, as if the way she felt for her daughter was already so immense it was seeping out of her.

Or maybe that was just exhaustion. It had been a long labor, almost twenty hours. Even with the epidural, which—surprise!—you didn't get the moment you walked into the hospital, it had been hard.

Adriano made a low, rough noise of agreement, his eyes

suspiciously bright. Poor guy. He broke bones without even blinking, but one baby girl brought him to tears.

She caught his hand with her free one, the two of them sharing an infatuated smile. They'd done it. They were parents. And they couldn't be more in love. With each other or with Gabriela.

Then Lil ruined the moment by yawning. God, she was tired.

Adriano scooped Gabriela up, rocking her as she settled into his arms. When the nurse had first handed his daughter to him, he'd begun to sway automatically, his body instinctively trying to soothe his baby. He was going to be such a wonderful dad—he was already a natural.

"Do you want some water?" he asked. The nurse had told Lil to drink a liter of water for every nursing session, so Lil knew what Adriano would be bugging her about for the next few weeks.

But he worried because he loved.

Lil shook her head, rubbed her eyes. "I'm so tired. And so hungry. All I want to do it stare at her, eat a pizza, and take a nap." Where was Luke with her pizza? She hadn't eaten since she'd gotten to the hospital, and she'd just gone through the most physically draining experience of her life. She deserved some pizza after all that.

"Luke's on his way." But most of Adriano's attention was on the baby. The expression on his face, so open, so wondering, so filled with love, made her heart swell.

Thank God he knocked me up.

They'd spent the past few months building the bull operation—a transcontinental bull operation, even flying to Brazil to look at ranches. It had been tough, compromising with Adriano, juggling that and the stock operations and trying to get everything together before the baby came. Tough, but enjoyable. They were making it work.

And in Mato Grosso do Sul, Adriano had been so happy. It had been a joy to see him there, surrounded by family. Lil had met his mother, whom she found utterly delightful. And who had been moved up the transplant list—in two months, Lil and Adriano would fly back to be by her side during the ordeal. But after that, his mother would likely have a good, long life, her children and grandchildren surrounding her for many years.

Her family had all come earlier to coo over Gabriela, but now they were alone, their first night together as a family. Adriano would have to sleep in the chair next to Lil's bed, but she guessed that this was only the first of many nights with little to no sleep for them.

She yawned again, her eyes fluttering closed. *Speaking of sleep...*

No, wait. She had a pizza coming. She'd never done more to earn a meal in her life.

"You can sleep," Adriano said. "I've got her."

Lil smiled fondly. Yes, he did. She had nothing to worry about with Gabriela in his arms.

"She's so beautiful." Lil felt like she could never say that enough, could never fully impress on everyone how remarkable this baby was.

"She is. And so is her mama." He caught up her left hand and studied it. "When do you think the swelling will go down?"

"Hey! That's a hell of a thing to ask a woman who's just had a baby." Her indignation was partly deflated by the sleepiness in her voice.

He rubbed his thumb across her knuckles, let his smile

stretch wide. "I only want to know when the ring I bought you will fit."

She blinked at him. Of all the times to bring this up... Only, maybe it was exactly the right time. "Are you proposing to me? Because we've already got something permanent right there."

The most perfect piece of permanence ever made.

"I know. But I want to give you more." The words were filled with love, so much that she didn't understand how the syllables could hold it all.

She put her lips to his, gave him a soft kiss. "First the baby, then a marriage. We've done everything ass backward, haven't we?"

He kissed her back. "Maybe. But it was the perfect way for us."

She wouldn't have wanted them to get here any other way than that.

WANT MORE HOT COWBOY ROMANCE? Pick up *Rescued by Her Fire Fighter,* the next in A Cowboy of Her Own! Keep reading for a sneak peek!